The yellowbacks... classics of popular fiction

The yellowjackets or yellowbacks were a great series of bestselling adventure and crime thrillers that had its origins in the mid to late 19th century following on from the 'penny dreadfuls'. They virtually began the mass market revolution of the early 20th century with a clear standard format and imprint/series livery (what would today be called branding). Hodder & Stoughton published the yellowjackets in two main series with series run dates of: 1923-1939 and later 1949-1957.

As the tagline ('where thrillers really began') on the back cover implies, the imprint and series focused on thrillers that were the bestsellers of their time. This current reissue or retro revival if you will, brings back many of these masterpieces, now classics in their own way and extends it further by including key titles from that period that were either great crime or thriller or even general commercial fiction (including sub-genres of noir, horror, gothic, romance, westerns, etc.) influences of their time. There are some perennial favourites and many rarities either lost or not easily available being revived in the current series. Writers and characters ranged from adventure heroes like Bulldog Drummond, Allan Quatermain, Richard Hannay or the Saint through thriller grandmasters Edgar Wallace and E. Phillips Oppenheim, crime and mystery maestros like Patricia Wentworth, G.K. Chesterton, Agatha Christie and the Detection club, to western and swashbucklers like Zane Grey, Max Brand, Captain Blood and even romance or general fiction classics like Hermina Black, Denise Robins, Marie Corelli or Stella Morton. These were books that had storytelling at their heart and always entertained.

The yellowbacks had both hardback (with varying design elements) and paperback (which built the series look) versions with the latter still carrying the imprint 'yellowjacket'. The current reissues pay tribute to both and use an amalgam of elements from both editions while retaining the complete yellow (or 'mustard-plaster') livery with the author's name in blue beveled type with a 'simulated emboss' effect and a white outer 'outline', and the book title in black. These reissues retain the distinctive size of the original mass market paperback and follow the three main category variations—the thrillers (crime, westerns, mystery, adventure) had blue lettering for the author's name, while Romance and softer general fiction had red; and other categories like humour had green.

For more details and a full list of titles visit https://www.hachetteindia.com/home/yellowbacks

THE GIRL AT CENTRAL

THE GIRL AT CENTRAL

Geraldine Bonner (1870–1930) was an American author, born on Staten Island, New York. Her father, John Bonner was a journalist and historical writer. As a child, Geraldine Bonner moved to Colorado where she lived in mining camps. After moving to San Francisco, California, she worked at a newspaper, the *Argonaut*, in 1887, and subsequently. She wrote the *novel Hard Pan* (1900) and used the name Hard Pan as a pseudonym.

Bonner wrote short stories which were published in *Collier's Weekly, Harper's Weekly, Harper's Monthly,* and *Lippincott's.*

THE GIRL AT CENTRAL

Geraldine Bonner

HODDER AND STOUGHTON
YELLOW JACKET
hachette

The Girl at Central
First published in 1915 by D. Appleton and Company New York and London

This Hodder Yellowback edition © Hachette India 2023
(Registered Name: Hachette Book Publishing India Pvt. Ltd.)
An Hachette UK Company www.hachetteindia.com

1

The texts in these editions in most cases have been reprinted as is, with minimal editorial changes and by and large no bowdlerizing for political correctness; though in some editions, a few words and phrases considered archaic, or those considered offensive now, along with archaic punctuation may have been modified in places to make the text more accessible to today's readers. The narratives, language, beliefs, social mores and/or cultural depictions, in these volumes are a reflection of their times and must be viewed as such. They may also contain certain cultural, racial and gender prejudices and stereotypes that may be outdated or clearly wrong then and wrong today; but their removal would be tantamount to claiming these prejudices never existed. The Publisher does not endorse or support those depictions or stereotypes; and these books have been made available for a discerning audience that will read it for entertainment value and a chronicle/record of popular fiction of past times.

Cover design by Priya Singh adapted from the original classic yellowjacket by Hodder & Stoughton.

Cover illustration by Ishan Trivedi.

Series note: Some of the books in the series (unless otherwise credited) may have cover or inside illustrations from the original yellowbacks or early editions, and while full restoration has been attempted, some images may be grainy or faded due to the condition of the original material. The end notes or bonus material or blurb details may have been sourced from the public domain or free use publications such as Wikipedia and attribution is hereby made also allowing similar free use reproduction from here. Sources requiring further specific attribution may write in and further detailing and/or corrections shall be made in subsequent printings/editions.

Reprint specifications may be subject to change including but not limited to finishes, paper, colour sections.

ISBN: 978-93-5731-070-3

Hachette Book Publishing India Pvt. Ltd.
4th & 5th Floors, Corporate Centre,
Plot No. 94, Sector 44, Gurugram - 122 003, India

Typeset in Electra LT STD 10/12.5 pt by Manipal Technologies Limited, Manipal

Printed and bound in India by Manipal Technologies Limited, Manipal

MIX
Paper from responsible sources
FSC™ C043100

CONTENTS

I

Poor Sylvia Hesketh! Even now, after this long time, I can't think of it without a shudder, without a comeback of the horror of those days after the murder. You remember it – the Hesketh mystery? And mystery it surely was, baffling, as it did, the police and the populace of the whole state. For who could guess why a girl like that, rich, beautiful, without a care or an enemy, should be done to death as she was. Think of it – at five o'clock sitting with her mother taking tea in the library at Mapleshade and that same night found dead – murdered – by the side of a lonesome country road, a hundred and eighteen miles away.

It's the story of this that I'm going to tell here, and as you'll get a good deal of me before I'm through, I'd better, right now at the start, introduce myself.

I'm Molly Morganthau, day operator in the telephone exchange at Longwood, New Jersey, twenty-three years old, dark, slim, and as for my looks – well, put them down as "medium" and let it go at that. My name's Morganthau because my father was a Polish Jew – a piece worker on pants – but my two front names, Mary McKenna, are after my mother, who was from County Galway, Ireland. I was raised in an East Side tenement, but I went steady to the Grammar school and through the High and I'm not throwing bouquets at myself when I say I made a good record. That's how I come to be nervy enough to write this story – but you'll see for yourself. Only just keep in mind that I'm more at home in front of a switchboard than at a desk.

I've supported myself since I was sixteen, my father dying then, and my mother – God rest her blessed memory! – two years later. First I was in a department store and then in the Telephone Company. I haven't a relation in the country and if I had I wouldn't have asked a nickel off them. I'm that kind, independent and – but that's enough about me.

Now for you to rightly get what I'm going to tell I'll have to begin with a description of Longwood village and the country round about. I've made a sort of diagram – it isn't drawn to scale but it gives the general effect, all right – and with that and what I'll describe you can get an idea of the lay of the land, which you have to have to understand things.

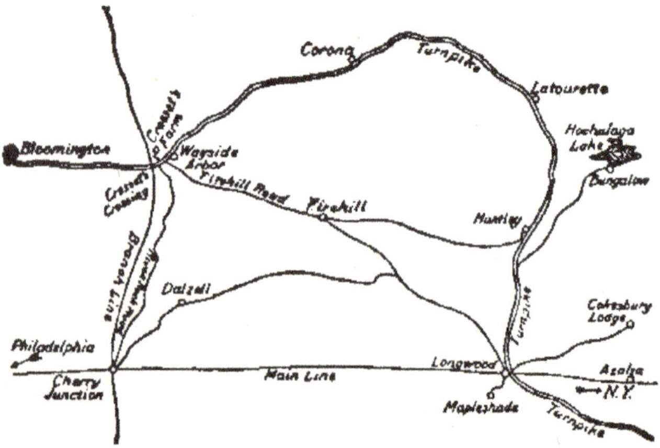

Longwood's in New Jersey, a real picturesque village of a thousand inhabitants. It's a little over an hour from New York by the main line and here and there round it are country places, mostly fine ones owned by rich people. There are some farms too, and along the railway and the turnpike are other villages. My exchange is the central office for a good radius of country, taking in Azalea, twenty-five miles above us on the main line, and running its wires out in a big circle to the scattered houses and the crossroad settlements. It's on Main Street, opposite the station, and from my chair at the switchboard I can see the platform and the trains as they come down from Cherry Junction or up from New York. It's sixty miles from Longwood to the Junction where you get the branch line that goes off to the North, stopping at other stations, mostly for the farm people, and where, when you get to Hazelmere, you can connect with an express for Philadelphia. Also you can keep right on from the Junction and get to Philadelphia that way, which is easier, having no changes and better trains.

When I was first transferred from New York – it's over two years now – I thought I'd die of the lonesomeness of it. At night, looking out of my window – I lived over Galway's Elite Millinery Parlors on Lincoln Street – across those miles and miles of country with a few lights dotted here and there, I felt like I was cast on a desert island. After a while I got used to it and that first spring when the woods began to get a faint greenish look and I'd wake up and hear birds twittering in the elms along the street – hold on! I'm getting sidetracked. It's going to be hard at first to keep myself out, but just be patient, I'll do it better as I go along.

The county turnpike goes through Longwood, and then sweeps away over the open country between the estates and the farms and now and then a village – Huntley, Latourette, Corona – strung out along it like beads on a string. A hundred and fifty miles off it reaches Bloomington, a big town with hotels and factories and a jail. About twenty miles before it gets to Bloomington it crosses the branch line near Cresset's Farm. There's a little sort of station there – just an open shed – called Cresset's Crossing, built for the Cresset Farm people, who own a good deal of land in that vicinity. Not far from Cresset's Crossing, about a half mile apart, the Riven Rock Road from the Junction and the Firehill Road from Jack Reddy's estate run into the turnpike.

This is the place, I guess, where I'd better tell about Jack Reddy, who was such an important figure in the Hesketh mystery and who – I get red now when I write it – was such an important figure to me.

A good ways back – about the time of the Revolution – the Reddy family owned most of the country round here. Bit by bit they sold it off till in old Mr Reddy's time – Jack's father – all they had left was the Firehill property and Hochalaga Lake, a big body of water, back in the hills beyond Huntley. Firehill is an old-fashioned stone house, built by Mr Reddy's grandfather. It got its name from a grove of maples on the top of a mound that in the autumn used to turn red and orange and look like the hillock was in a blaze. The name, they say, came from the Indian days and so did Hochalaga, though what that stands for I don't know. The Reddys had had lots of offers for the lake but never would sell it. They had a sort of little shack there and before Jack's time, when there were no automobiles, used to make horseback excursions to Hochalaga and stay for a few days. After the old people died and Jack came into the property everybody thought he'd sell the lake – several parties were after it for a summer resort – but he refused them all, had the shack built over into an up-to-date bungalow, and through the summer would have guests down from town, spending week-ends out there.

Now I'm telling everything truthful, for that's what I set out to do, and if you think I'm a fool you're welcome to and no back talk from me – but I was crazy about Jack Reddy. Not that he ever gave me cause; he's not that kind and neither am I. And let me say right here that there's not a soul ever knew it, he least of all. I guess no one would have been more surprised than the owner of Firehill if he'd known that the Longwood telephone girl most had heart failure every time he passed the window of the Exchange.

I will say, to excuse myself, that there's few girls who wouldn't have put their hats straight and walked their prettiest when they saw him coming. Gee – he was a good looker! Like those advertisements for collars and shirts you see in the back of the magazines – you know the ones. But it wasn't that that got me. It was his ways, always polite, never fresh. If he'd meet me in the street he'd raise his hat as if I was the Queen of Sheba. And there wasn't any hanging round my switchboard and asking me to make dates for dinner in town. He was always jolly, but – a girl in a telephone exchange gets to know a lot – he was always a gentleman.

He lived at Firehill – forty miles from Longwood – with two old servants, David Gilsey and his wife, who'd been with his mother and just doted on him. But everybody liked him. There wasn't but one criticism I ever heard passed on him and that was that he had a violent temper. Casey, his chauffeur, told a story in the village of how one day, when they were passing a farm, they saw an Italian laborer prod a horse with a pitchfork. Before he knew, Mr Reddy was out of the car and over the fence and mashing the life out of that dago. It took Casey and the farmer to pull him off and they thought the dago'd be killed before they could.

There was talk in Longwood that he hadn't much money – much the way the Reddys had always had it – and was going to study law for a living. But he must have had some, for he kept up the house, and had two motors, one just a common roadster and the other a long gray racing car that he'd let out on the turnpike till he was twice arrested and once ran over a dog.

My, how well I got to know that car! When I first came I only saw it at long intervals. Then – just as if luck was on my side – I began to see it oftener and oftener, slowing down as it came along Main Street, swinging round the corner, jouncing across the tracks, and dropping out of sight behind the houses at the head of Maple Lane.

"What's bringing Jack Reddy in this long way so often?" people would say at first.

Then, after a while, when they'd see the gray car, they'd look sly at each other and wink.

There's one good thing about having a crush on a party that's never thought any more about you than if you were the peg he hangs his hat on – it doesn't hurt so bad when he falls in love with his own kind of girl.

And that brings me – as if I was in the gray car speeding down Maple Lane – to Mapleshade and the Fowlers and Sylvia Hesketh.

II

About a mile from Longwood, standing among ancient, beautiful trees, is Mapleshade, Dr Dan Fowler's place.

It was once a farmhouse, over a century old, but two and a half years ago when Dr Fowler bought it he fixed it all up, raised the roof, built on a servants' wing and a piazza with columns and turned the farm buildings into a garage. Artists and such people say it's the prettiest place in this part of the State, and it certainly is a picture, especially in summer, with the lawns mown close as velvet and the flower-beds like bits of carpet laid out to air.

The Doctor bought a big bit of land with it – I don't know how many hundred acres – so the house, though it's not far from the village, is kind of secluded and shut away. You get to it by Maple Lane, a little winding road that runs between trees caught together with wild grape and Virginia creeper. In summer they're like green walls all draped over with the vines and in winter they turn into a rustling gray hedge, woven so close it's hard to see through. About ten minutes' walk from the gate of Mapleshade there's a pine that was struck by lightning and stands up black and bare.

When the house was finished the Doctor, who was a bachelor, married Mrs Hesketh, a widow lady accounted rich, and he and she came there as bride and groom with her daughter, Sylvia Hesketh. I hadn't come yet, but from what I've heard, there was gossip about them from the start. What

I can say from my own experience is that I'd hardly got my grip unpacked when I began to hear of the folks at Mapleshade.

They lived in great style with a housekeeper, a butler and a French maid for the ladies. In the garage were three automobiles, Mrs Fowler's limousine, the Doctor's car and a dandy little roadster that belonged to Miss Sylvia. Neither she nor the Doctor bothered much with the chauffeur. They left him to take Mrs Fowler round and drove themselves, the joke going that if Miss Sylvia ever went broke she could qualify for a chauffeur's job.

After a while the story came out that it wasn't Mrs Fowler who was so rich but Miss Hesketh. The late Mr Hesketh had only left his wife a small fortune, willing the rest – millions, it was said – to his daughter. She was a minor – nineteen – and the trustees of the estate allowed her a lot of money for her maintenance, thirty thousand a year they had it in Longwood.

In spite of the grand way they lived there wasn't much company at Mapleshade. Anne Hennessey, the housekeeper, told me Mrs Fowler was so dead in love with her husband she didn't want the bother of entertaining people. And the Doctor liked a quiet life. He'd been a celebrated surgeon in New York but had retired only for consultations and special cases now and again. He was very good to the people round about, and would come in and help when our little Dr Pease, or Dr Graham, at the Junction, were up against something serious. I'll never forget when Mick Donahue, the station agent's boy, got run over by Freight No. 22. But I'm sidetracked again. Anyhow, the Doctor amputated the leg and little Mick's stumping round on a wooden pin almost as good as ever.

But even so they weren't liked much. They held their heads very high, Mrs Fowler driving through the village like it was Fifth Avenue, sending the chauffeur into the shops and not at all affable to the tradespeople. The Doctor wouldn't trouble to give you so much as a nod, just stride along looking straight ahead. When the story got about that he'd lost most of the money he'd made doctoring I didn't bear any resentment, seeing it was worry that made him that way.

But Miss Sylvia was made on a different measure. My, but she was a winner! Even after I knew what brought Jack Reddy in from Firehill so often I couldn't be set against her. Jealous I might be of a girl like myself, but not of one who was the queen bee of the hive.

She was a beauty from the ground up – a blonde with hair like corn silk that she wore in a loose, fluffy knot with little curly ends hanging on her neck. Her face was pure pink and white, the only dark thing in it her big brown eyes, that were as clear and soft as a baby's. And she was a great dresser, always the latest novelty, and looking prettier in each one. Mrs Galway'd say to me, with her nose caught up, scornful,

"To my mind it's not refined to advertise your wealth on your back."

But I didn't worry, knowing Mrs Galway'd have advertised hers if she'd had the wealth or a decent shaped back to advertise it on, which she hadn't, being round-shouldered.

There was none of the haughty ways of her parents about Miss Sylvia. When she'd come into the exchange to send a call (a thing that puzzled me first but I soon caught on) she'd always stop and have a pleasant word with me. On bright afternoons I'd see her pass on horseback, straight as an arrow, with a man's hat on her golden hair. She'd always have a smile for everyone, touching her hat brim real sporty with the end of her whip. Even when she was in her motor, speeding down Main Street, she'd give you a hail as jolly as if she was your college chum.

Sometimes she'd be alone but generally there was a man along. There were a lot of them hanging round her, which was natural, seeing she had everything to draw them like a candle drawing moths. They'd come and go from town and now and then stay over Sunday at the Longwood Inn – it's a swell little place done up in the Colonial style – and you'd see them riding and walking with her, very devoted. At first everybody thought her parents were agreeable to all the attention she was getting. It wasn't till the Mapleshade servants began to talk too much that we heard the Fowlers, especially the Doctor, didn't like it.

I hadn't known her long before I began to notice something that interested me. A telephone girl sees so many people and hears such a lot of confidential things on the wire, that she gets to know more than most about what I suppose you'd call human nature. It's a study that's always attracted me and in Miss Sylvia's case there was a double attraction – I was curious about her for myself and I was curious about her because of Jack Reddy.

What I noticed was that she was so different with men to what she was with women – affable to both, but it was another kind of affability. I've seen considerably many girls trying to throw their harpoons into men and doing it too, but they were in the booby class beside Miss Sylvia. She was what the novelists call a coquette, but she was that dainty and sly about it that I don't believe any of the victims knew it. It wasn't what she said, either; more the way she looked and the soft, sweet manner she had, as if she thought more of the chap she was talking to than anybody else in the world. She'd be that way to one in my exchange and the next day I'd see her just the same with another in the drugstore.

It made me uneasy. Even if the man you love doesn't love you, you don't want to see him fooled. But I said nothing – I'm the close sort – and it wasn't till I came to be friends with Anne Hennessey that I heard the inside facts about the family at Mapleshade.

Anne Hennessey was a Canadian and a fine girl. She was a lady and had a lady's job – seventy-five a month and her own bathroom – and being the real thing she didn't put on any airs, but when she liked me made right up to me and we soon were pals. After work hours I'd sometimes go up to her at Mapleshade or she'd come down to me over the Elite.

I remember it was in my room one spring evening – me lying on the bed and Anne sitting by the open window – that she began to talk about the Fowlers. She was not one to carry tales, but I could see she had something on her mind and for the first time she loosened up. I was picking over a box of chocolates and I didn't give her a hint how keen I was to hear, acting like the candies had the best part of my attention. She began by saying the Doctor and Miss Sylvia didn't get on well.

"That's just like a novel," I answered, "the heroine's stepfather's always her natural enemy."

"He's not that in this case," said Anne – she speaks English fine, like the teachers in the High – "I'm sure he means well by her, but they can't get on at all, they're always quarreling."

"There's many a gilded home hides a tragedy. What do they fight about?"

"Things she does he disapproves of. She's very spoiled and self-willed. No one's ever controlled her and she resents it from him."

"What's he disapprove of?"

Anne didn't answer right off, looking thoughtful out of the window. Then she said slow as if she was considering her words:

"I'm going to tell you, Molly, because I know you're no gossip and can be trusted, and the truth is, I'm worried. I don't like the situation up at Mapleshade."

I swung my feet on to the floor and sat up on the edge of the bed, nibbling at a chocolate almond.

"Here's where I get dumb," I said, sort of casual to encourage her.

"Sylvia Hesketh's a girl that needs a strong hand over her and there's no one has it. Her father's dead, her mother – poor Mrs Fowler's only a grown-up baby ready to say black is white if her husband wants her to – and Dr Fowler's trying to do it and he's going about it all wrong. You see," she said, turning to me very serious, "it's not only that she's head-strong and extravagant but she's an incorrigible flirt."

"Is there a place in the back of the book where you can find out what incorrigible means?" I said.

Anne smiled, but not as if she felt like it.

"Uncontrollable, irrepressible. Her mother – Mrs Fowler's ready to tell me anything and everything – says she's always been like that. And, of course, with her looks and her fortune the men are around her like flies round honey."

"Why does the Doctor mind that?"

"I suppose he wouldn't mind if they just came to Mapleshade or Longwood. But – that's what the quarreling's about – he's found out that she meets them in town, goes to lunch and the matinée with them."

"Excuse me, but I've left my etiquette book on the piano. What's wrong about going to the matinée or to lunch?"

"Nothing's really wrong. Mind you, Molly, I know Sylvia through and through and there's no harm in her – it's just the bringing-up and the spoiling and the admiration. But, of course, in her position, a girl doesn't go about that way without a chaperone. The Doctor's perfectly right to object."

I was looking down, pretending to hunt over the box.

"Who does she go with?" I said.

"Oh, there are several. A man named Carisbrook—" I'd seen him often, a swell guy in white spats and a high hat – "and a young lawyer called Dunham and Ben Robinson, a Canadian like me. People see her with them and tell the doctor and there's a row."

I looked into the box as careful as if I was searching for a diamond.

"Ain't Mr Reddy one of the happy family?" I asked. "Ah, here's the last almond!"

"Oh, of course, young Reddy. I think it would be a good thing if she married him. Everybody says he's a fine fellow, and I tell you now, Molly, with Sylvia so willful and the doctor so domineering and Mrs Fowler being pulled to pieces between them, things at Mapleshade can't go on long the way they are."

That was in May. At the end of June the Fowlers went to Bar Harbor with all their outfit for the summer. After that Jack Reddy didn't come into Longwood much. I heard that he was spending a good deal of his time at the bungalow at Hochalaga Lake, and I did see him a few times meeting his company at the train – he had some week-end parties out there – and bringing them back in the gray car.

At the end of September the Fowlers came home. It was great weather, clear and crisp, with the feel of frost in the air. Most everybody was out of doors and I saw Sylvia often, sometimes on horseback, sometimes driving her motor. She was prettier than ever for the change and seemed like she couldn't stay in the house. I'd see her riding toward home in the red light of the sunset, and as I walked back from work her car often would flash past me, speeding through the early dark toward Maple Lane.

Anne said they'd had a fairly peaceful summer and she hoped they were going to get on better. There had only been one row – that was about a man who was up at Bar Harbor and had met Sylvia and paid her a good deal of attention. The Doctor had been very angry as he disapproved of the man – Cokesbury was his name.

"Cokesbury!" I cut in surprised – we were in Anne's room that evening – "why, he belongs round here."

Anne had heard that and wanted to know what I knew about him, which I'll write down in this place as it seems to fit in and has to be told somewhere.

When I first came to Longwood, Mr and Mrs Cokesbury were living on their estate, Cokesbury Lodge, about twenty-five miles from us, near Azalea. They had been in France for a year previous to that, then come back and taken up their residence in Mr Cokesbury's country seat, and it was shortly after that Mrs Cokesbury died there, leaving three children. For a while the widower stayed on with nurses and governesses to look after the poor motherless kids. Then, the eldest boy taking sick and nearly dying, he decided to send them to his wife's parents, who had wanted them since Mrs Cokesbury's death.

So the establishment at the Lodge was broken up and Mr Cokesbury went to live in town. There were rumors that the house was to be sold, but in the spring Sands, the Pullman conductor, told me that Mr Cokesbury had been down several times, staying over Sunday and had said he had given up the idea of selling the place. He told Sands he couldn't get his price for it and what was the sense of selling at a loss, especially when he could come out there and get a breath of country air when he was scorched up with the city heat?

I'd passed the house one day in August when I was on an auto ride with some friends. It was a big, rambling place with a lot of dismal-looking pines around it, about five miles from Azalea and with no near neighbors. Mr Cokesbury only kept one car – he'd had several when his wife was there – and used to drive himself down from the Lodge to the station, leave his car in the Azalea garage, and drive himself back the next time he came. He had no servants or caretaker, which he didn't need, as, after Mrs Cokesbury's death, all the valuable things had been taken out of the house and sent to town for storage.

It gave me a jar to hear that Sylvia Hesketh – who, in my mind, was as good as engaged to Jack Reddy – would have anything to do with him. I'd never seen him, but I'd heard a lot that wasn't to his credit. He hadn't been good to his wife – everybody said she was a real lady – but was the gay, wild kind, and not young, either. Anne said he was forty if he was a day. When I asked her what Sylvia could see in an old gink like that, she just shrugged up her shoulders and said, who could tell – Sylvia was made that way. She was like some woman whose name I can't remember who sat on a rock and sang to the sailors till they got crazy and jumped into the water.

My head was full of these things one glorious afternoon toward the end of October when – it being my holiday – I started out for a walk through the woods. The woods cover the hills behind the village and they're grand, miles and miles of them. But wait! There was a little thing that happened, by the way, that's worth telling, for it gave me a premonition – is that the word? Or, maybe, I'd better say connected up with what was in my mind.

I was walking slow down Main Street when opposite the postoffice I saw all the loafers and most of the tradespeople lined up in a ring staring at a bunch of those dago acrobats that go about the State all summer doing stunts on a bit of carpet. I'd seen them often – chaps in dirty pink tights walking on their hands and rolling round in knots – and I wouldn't have stopped but I got a glimpse of little Mick Donahue stumping round the outside trying to squeeze in and trying not to cry because he couldn't. So I stopped and hoisted him up for a good view, telling the men in front to break a way for the kid to see.

There was a dago scraping on a fiddle and while the acrobats were performing on their carpet, a big bear with a little, brown, shriveled-up man holding it by a chain, was dancing. And when I got my first look at that bear, in spite of all my worry I burst out laughing, for, dancing away there solemn and slow, it was the dead image of Dr Fowler.

You'd have laughed yourself if you'd seen it – that is, if you'd known the Doctor. There was something so like him in its expression – sort of gloomy and thoughtful – and its little eyes set up high in its head and looking angry at the crowd as if it despised them. When its master jerked the chain and shouted something in a foreign lingo it hitched up its lip like it was trying to smile, and that sideways grin, as if it didn't feel at all pleasant, was just the way the Doctor'd smile when he came into the Exchange and gave me a number.

It fascinated me and I stood staring with little Mick sitting on my arm, just loving it all, his dirty little fist clasped round a penny. Then the music stopped and one of the acrobats came round with a hat and little Mick gave a great sigh as if he was coming out of a dream. "If you hadn't come, Molly, I'd have missed it," he said, looking into my face in that sweet wistful way sickly kids have, "and it's the last time they'll be round this year."

I kissed him and put him down and told the men as I squeezed out to keep him in the front or they'd hear from me. Then I walked off toward the woods thinking.

It was a funny idea I'd got into my head. I'd once read in a paper that when people looked like animals they resembled the animals in their dispositions – and I was wondering was Dr Fowler like a bear, grouchy and, when you crossed him, savage. Maybe it was because I'd been so worried, but it gave me a kind of chill. My thoughts went back to Mapleshade and I got one of those queer glimpses (like a curtain was lifted for a second and you could see things in the future) of trouble there – something dark – I don't know how to explain it, but it was as if I got a new line on the Doctor, as if the bear had made me see through the surface clear into him.

I tried to shake it off for I wanted to enjoy my afternoon in the woods. They are beautiful at that season, the trees full of colored leaves, and all quiet except for the rustlings of little animals round the roots. There's a road that winds along under the branches, and trails, soft under foot with fallen leaves and moss, that you can follow for miles.

I was coming down one of these, making no more noise than the squirrels, when just before it crossed the road I saw something and stopped. There, sitting side by side on a log, were Sylvia Hesketh and a man. Close to them, run off to the side, was a motor and near it tied to a tree a horse with a lady's saddle. Sylvia was in her riding dress, looking a picture, her eyes on the ground and slapping softly with her whip on the side of her boot. The man was leaning toward her, talking low and earnest and staring hard into her face.

To my knowledge I'd never seen him before, and it gave me a start – me saying, surprised to myself, "Hullo! here's another one?" He was a big, powerful chap, with a square, healthy looking face and wide shoulders on him like a prize fighter. He was dressed in a loose coat and knickerbockers and as he talked he had his hands spread out, one on each knee, great brown hands with hair on them. I was close enough to see that, but he was speaking so low and I was so scared that they'd see me and think I was spying, that I didn't hear what he was saying. The only one that saw me was the horse. It looked up sudden with its ears pricked, staring surprised with its soft gentle eyes.

I stole away like a robber, not making a speck of noise. All the joy I'd been taking in the walk under the colored leaves was gone. I felt kind of shriveled up inside – the way you feel when someone you love is sick. I couldn't bear to think that Jack Reddy was giving his heart to a girl who'd meet another man out in the woods and listen to him so coy and yet so interested.

As far as I can remember, that was a little over a month from the fatal day. All the rest of October and through the first part of November things went along quiet and peaceful. And then, suddenly, everything came together – quick like a blow.

III

For two days it had been raining, heavy straight rain. From my window at Galway's I could see the fields round the village full of pools and zigzags of water as if they'd been covered with a shiny gray veil that was suddenly pulled off and had caught in the stubble and been torn to rags. Saturday morning the weather broke. But the sky was still overcast and the air had that sort of warm, muggy breathlessness that comes after rain. That was November the twentieth.

It was eleven o'clock and I was sitting at the switchboard looking out at the streets, all puddles and ruts, when I got a call from the Dalzells' – a place near the Junction – for Mapleshade.

Now you needn't get preachy and tell me it's against the rules to listen – suspension and maybe discharge. I know that better than most. Didn't the roof over my head and the food in my mouth depend on me doing my work according to orders? But the fact is that at this time I was keyed up so high I'd got past being cautious. When a call came for Mapleshade I *listened*, listened hard, with all my ears. What did I expect to hear? I don't know exactly. It might have been Jack Reddy and it might have been Sylvia – oh, never mind what it was – just say I was curious and let it go at that.

So I lifted up the cam and took in the conversation.

It was a woman's voice – Mrs Dalzell's, I knew it well – and Dr Fowler's. Hers was trembly and excited:

"Oh, Dr Fowler, is that you? It's Mrs Dalzell, yes, near the Junction. My husband's very sick. We've had Dr Graham and he says it's appendicitis and there ought to be an operation – now, as soon as possible. *Do* you hear me?"

Then Dr Fowler, very calm and polite:

"Perfectly, madam."

"Oh, I'm so glad – I've been so *terribly* worried. It's so unexpected. Mr Dalzell's never had so much as a *cramp* before and now—"

"Just wait a minute, Mrs Dalzell," came the Doctor. "Let me understand. Graham recommends an operation, you say?"

"Yes, Dr Fowler, as soon as possible; something awful may happen if it's not done. And Dr Graham suggested you if you'd be so kind. I know it's a favor but I *must* have the best for my husband. *Won't* you come? Please, to oblige me."

Dr Fowler asked some questions which I needn't put down and said he'd come and if necessary operate. Then they talked about the best way for him to get there, the Doctor wanting to know if the main line to the Junction wouldn't be the quickest. But Mrs Dalzell said she'd been consulting the time tables and there'd be no train from Longwood to the Junction before two and if he wouldn't mind and would come in his auto by the Firehill Road he'd get there several hours sooner. He agreed to that and it wasn't fifteen minutes after he'd hung up that I saw him swing past my window in his car, driving himself.

Later on in the afternoon I got another call from the Dalzells' for Mapleshade and heard the Doctor tell Mrs Fowler that the operation had been a serious one and that he would stay there for the night and probably all the next day.

Before that second call, about two hours after the first one, there came another message for Mapleshade that before a week was out was in most every paper in the country and that lifted me right into the middle of the Hesketh mystery.

It was near one o'clock, an hour when work's slack round Longwood, everybody being either at their dinner or getting ready for it. The call was from a public pay station and was in a man's voice – a voice I didn't know, but that, because of my curiosity, I listened to as sharp as if it was my lover's asking me to marry him.

The man wanted to see Miss Sylvia and, after a short wait, I heard her answer, very gay and cordial and evidently knowing him at once without any questions. If she'd said one word to show who he was things afterward would have been very different, but there wasn't a single phrase that you could identify him by – all anyone could have caught was that they seemed to know each other very well.

He began by telling her it was a long time since he'd seen her and wanting to know if she'd come to town on Monday and take lunch with him at Sherry's and afterward go to a concert.

"Monday," she said very slow and soft, "the day after tomorrow? No, I can't make any engagement for Monday."

"Why not?" he asked.

She didn't answer right off and when she did, though her voice was so sweet, there was something sly and secret about it.

"I've something else to do."

"Can't you postpone it?"

She laughed at that, a little soft laugh that came bubbling through her words:

"No, I'm afraid not."

"Must be something very interesting."

"Um – maybe so."

"You're very mysterious – can't I be told what it is?"

"Why should you be told?"

That riled him, I could hear it in his voice.

"As a friend, or if I don't come under that head, as a fellow who's got the frosty mit and wants to know why."

"I don't think that's any reason. I have no engagement with you and I have with – someone else."

"Just tell me one thing – is it a man or a woman?"

She began to laugh again, and if I'd been the man at the other end of the wire that laugh would have made me wild.

"Which do you think?" she asked.

"I don't think, I *know*," and *I* knew that he was mad.

"Well, if you know," she said as sweet as pie, "I needn't tell you any more. I'll say goodbye."

"No," he shouted, "don't hang up – wait. What do you want to torment me for?" Then he got sort of coaxing, "It isn't kind to treat a fellow this way. Can't you tell me who it is?"

"No, that's a secret. You can't know a thing till I choose to tell you and I don't choose now."

"If I come over Sunday afternoon will you see me?"

"What time?"

"Any time you say – I'm your humble slave, as you know."

"I'm going out about seven."

"Where?"

"That's another secret."

I think a child listening to that conversation would have seen he was getting madder every minute and yet he was so afraid she'd cut him off that he had to keep it under and talk pleasant.

"Look here," he said, "I've something I want to say to you awfully. If I run over in my car and get there round six-thirty, can you see me for a few minutes?"

She didn't answer at once. Then she said slow as if she was undecided:

"Not at the house."

"I didn't mean at the house. Say in Maple Lane, by the gate. I won't keep you more than five or ten minutes."

"Six-thirty's rather late."

"Well, any time you say."

"Can't you be there exactly at six-fifteen?"

"If that's a condition."

"It is. If you're late you won't find me. I'll be gone" – she began to laugh again – "taking my secret with me."

"I'll be there on the dot."

"Very well, then, you can come – at the gate just as the clock marks one quarter after six. And, maybe, if you're good, I'll tell you the secret. Goodbye until then – try not to be too curious. It's a bad habit and I've seen signs of it in you lately. Goodbye."

Before he could say another word she'd disconnected.

I leaned back in my chair thinking it over. What was she up to? What was the secret? And who was the man? "Run over in his car" – that looked like someone from one of the big estates. How many of them *had* she buzzing round her?

And then, for all I was so downhearted, I couldn't help smiling to think of those two supposing they were talking so secluded and an East Side tenement girl taking it all in. Little did I guess then that me breaking the rules that way, instead of destroying me was going to—But that doesn't come in here.

And now I come to Sunday the twenty-first, a date I'll never forget.

It seemed to me afterward that Nature knew of the tragedy and prepared for it. The weather was duller and grayer than it had been on Saturday, not a breath of air stirring and the sky all mottled over with clouds, dark and heavy looking. A full moon was due and as I went to the Exchange I thought of the sweethearts that had dates to walk out in the moonlight and how disappointed they'd be.

Things weren't cheerful at the Exchange either. I found Minnie Trail, the night operator, as white as a ghost, saying she felt as if one of her sick headaches was coming on and if it did would I stay on over time? I knew those headaches – they ran along sometimes till eight or nine. I told her to go right home to bed and I'd hold the fort till she was able to relieve me. We often did turns like that, one for the other. It's one of the advantages of being in a small country office – no one picks on you for acting human.

About ten I had a call from Anne Hennessey. "Have you got anything on for this evening, Molly?"

"I have not. This is Longwood, not gay Paree."

"Then I'll come round to Galways, about seven and we'll go to the Gilt Edge for supper. I want to talk to you."

The Gilt Edge Lunch was where I took my meals, a nice clean little joint close to the office. But I didn't know when I'd get my supper that night, so I called back:

"That's all right, sister, but come to the Exchange. Minnie's head's on the blink and I'll stay on here late. Anything up?"

"Yes. I don't want to talk about it over the wire. There's been another row here – yesterday morning. It's horrible; I can't stand it. I'll tell you more this evening. So long."

I put my elbows on the table and sat forward thinking. If you'd asked me a year ago what I wanted most in the world I'd have said money. But I'd learnt considerable since then. "Money don't do it," I said to myself. "Look at the Fowlers with their jewels and their millions, scrapping till even the housekeeper on a fancy salary with a private bath can't stand it."

And there came up in my mind the memory of the East Side tenement where I was raised. I thought of my poor father, most killed with work, and my mother eking things out, doing housecleaning and never a hard word to each other or to me.

The night settled down early, black, dark and very still. At seven Anne Hennessey came in and sat down by the radiator, which was making queer noises with the heat coming up. Supper time's like dinner – few calls – so I turned round in my chair, ready for a good talk, and asked about the trouble at Mapleshade.

"Oh, it was another quarrel yesterday morning at breakfast and with Harper, the butler, hearing every word. He said it was the worst they'd ever had. He's a self-respecting, high-class servant and was shocked."

"Sylvia and the Doctor again?"

"Yes, and poor Mrs Fowler crying behind the coffee pot."

"The same old subject?"

"Oh, of course. It's young Reddy this time. Sylvia's been out a good deal this autumn in her car; several times she's been gone nearly the whole day. When the Doctor questioned her she'd either be evasive or sulky. On Friday someone told him they'd seen her far up on the turnpike with Jack Reddy in his racer."

I fired up, I couldn't help it.

"Why should he be mad about that? Isn't Mr Reddy good enough for her?"

"*I* think he is. I told you before I thought the best thing she could do would be to marry him. But—" she looked round to see that no one was coming in—"don't say a word of what I'm going to tell you. I have no right to repeat what I hear as an employee but I'm worried and don't know what's the best thing to do. Mrs Fowler has as good as told me that her husband's lost all his money and it's Sylvia's that's running Mapleshade. And what *I* think is that the Doctor doesn't want her to marry *anyone*. It isn't her he minds losing; it's thirty thousand a year."

"But when she comes of age she can do what she wants and if he makes it so disagreeable she won't want to live there."

"That's two years off yet. He may recoup himself in that time."

"Oh, I see. But he can't do any good by fighting with her."

"Molly, you're a wise little woman. *Of course* he can't, but he doesn't know it. He treats that hot-headed, high-spirited girl like a child of five. Mark my words, there's going to be trouble at Mapleshade."

I thought of the telephone message I'd overheard the day before and it came to me suddenly what "the secret" might be. Could Sylvia have been planning to run away? I didn't say anything – it's natural to me and you get trained along those lines in the telephone business – and I sat turning it over in my mind as Anne went on.

"I'd leave tomorrow only I'm so sorry for Mrs Fowler. She's as helpless as a baby and seems to cling to me. The other day she told me about her first marriage – how her husband didn't care for her but was crazy about Sylvia – that's why he left her almost all his money."

I wasn't listening much, still thinking about "the secret." If she *was* running away was she going alone or with Jack Reddy? My eyes were fixed on the window and I saw, without noticing particular, the down train from the city draw into the station, and then Jim Donahue run along the platform swinging a lantern. As if I was in a dream I could hear Anne:

"I call it an unjust will – only two hundred thousand dollars to his wife and five millions to his daughter. But if Sylvia dies first, all the money goes back to Mrs Fowler."

The train pulled out, snorting like a big animal. Jim disappeared, then presently I saw him open the depot door and come slouching across the street. I knew he was headed for the Exchange, thinking Minnie Trail was there, he being a widower with a crush on Minnie.

He came in and, after he'd got over the shock of seeing me, turned to Anne and said:

"I just been putting your young lady on the train."

Anne gave a start and stared at him.

"Miss Sylvia?" she said.

"That's her," said Jim, warming his coat tails at the radiator.

I could see Anne was awful surprised and was trying to hide it.

"Who was she with?" she asked.

"No one. She went up alone and said she was going to be away for a few days. Where's she going?"

Anne gave me a look that said, "Keep your mouth shut," and turned quiet and innocent to Jim. "Just for a visit to friends. She's always visiting people in New York and Philadelphia."

Jim stayed round a while gabbing with us, and then went back to the station. When the door shut on him we stared at each other with our eyes as round as marbles.

"Oh, Molly," Anne said, almost in a whisper, "it's just what I've been afraid of."

"You think she's lighting out?"

"Yes – don't you see, the Doctor being at the Dalzells' has given her the chance."

"Where would she go to?"

"How do I know? Heaven send she hasn't done anything foolish. But this morning she sent Virginie, that French woman, up to the village for something – on Sunday when all the shops are shut. The housemaid told me they'd been trying to find out what it was and Virginie wouldn't tell. Oh, dear, *could* she have gone off with someone?"

We were talking it over in low voices when a call came. It was from Mapleshade to the Dalzells'. As I made the connection I whispered to Anne what it was and she whispered back, "Listen."

I did. It was from Mrs Fowler, all breathless and almost crying. She asked for the Doctor and when he came burst out:

"Oh, Dan, something's happened – something dreadful. Sylvia's run away."

I could hear the Doctor's voice, small and distant but quite clear:

"Go slow now, Connie, it's hard to hear you. Did you say *Sylvia'd run away*?"

Then Mrs Fowler said, trying to speak slower:

"Yes, with Jack Reddy. We've been hunting for her and we've just found a letter from him in her desk. Do you hear – her desk, in the top drawer? It told her to meet him at seven in the Lane and go with him in his car to Bloomington."

"Bloomington? That's a hundred and fifty miles off."

"I can't help how far off it is. That's where the letter said he was going to take her. It said they'd go by the turnpike to Bloomington and be married there. And we can't find Virginie – they've evidently taken her with them."

"I see – by the turnpike, did you say?"

"Yes. Can't you go up there and meet them and bring her back?"

"Yes – keep cool now, I'll head them off. What time did you say they left?"

"The letter said he'd meet her in the Lane at seven and it's a little after eight now. Have you time to get up there and catch them?"

"Time? – to burn. On a night like this Reddy can't get round to the part of the pike where I'll strike it under three and a half to four hours."

"But can you go – can you leave your case?"

"Yes – Dalzell's improving. Graham can attend to it. Now don't get excited, I'll have her back some time tonight. And not a word to anybody. We don't want this to get about. We'll have to shut the mouth of that fool of a French woman, but I'll see to that later. Don't see anyone. Go to your room and say nothing."

Just as the message was finished Minnie Trail came in. I made the record of it and then got up asking her, as natural as you please, how she felt. Anne did the same and you'd never have thought to hear us sympathizing with her that we were just bursting to get outside.

When we did we walked slow down the street, me telling her what I'd heard. All the time I was speaking I was thinking of Sylvia and Jack Reddy tearing away through that still, black night, flying along the pale line of the road, flashing past the lights of farms and country houses, swinging down between the rolling hills and out by the open fields, till they'd see the glow of Bloomington low down in the sky.

It was Anne who brought me back to where I was. She suddenly stopped short, staring in front of her and then turned to me:

"Why, how can she be eloping with Reddy by the turnpike when Jim Donahue saw her get on the train?"

IV

When I come to the next day I can't make my story plain if I only tell what I saw and heard. I didn't even pick up the most important message in the tragedy. It came at half-past nine that night through the Corona Exchange and was sent from a pay station so there was no record of it, only Jack Reddy's word – but I'm going too fast; that belongs later.

What I've got to do is to piece things together as I got them from the gossip in the village, from the inquest, and from the New York papers. All I ask of you is to remember that I'm up against a stunt that's new to me and that I'm trying to get it over as clear as I can.

The best way is for me to put down first Sylvia's movements on that tragic Sunday.

About five in the afternoon Sylvia and Mrs Fowler had tea in the library. When that was over – about half-past – Sylvia went away, saying she was going to her room to write letters, and her mother retired to hers for the nap she always took before dinner. What happened between then and the time when Mrs Fowler sent the message to the Doctor I heard from Anne Hennessey. It was this way:

They had dinner late at Mapleshade – half-past seven – and when Sylvia didn't come down Mrs Fowler sent up Harper to call her. He came back saying she wasn't in her room, and Mrs Fowler, getting uneasy, went up herself, sending Harper to find Virginie Dupont. It wasn't long before they discovered that neither Sylvia nor Virginie were in the house.

When she realized this Mrs Fowler was terribly upset. Sylvia's room was in confusion, the bureau drawers pulled out, the closet doors open. Anne not being there, Harper, who was scared at Mrs Fowler's excitement, called Nora Magee, the chambermaid. She was a smart girl and saw pretty quickly that Sylvia had evidently left. The toilet things were gone from the dresser; the jewelry case was open and empty, only for a few old pieces of no great value. It was part of Nora's job to do up the room and she knew where Sylvia's Hudson seal coat hung in one of the closets. A glance showed her that was gone, also a gold-fitted bag that the Doctor had given his stepdaughter on her birthday.

All the servants knew of the quarreling and its cause and while Mrs Fowler was moaning and hunting about helplessly, Nora went to the desk and opened it. There, lying careless as if it had been thrown in in a hurry, was Jack Reddy's letter. She gave a glance at it and handed it to Mrs Fowler. With the letter in her hand Mrs Fowler ran downstairs and telephoned to the Doctor.

The poor lady was in a terrible way and when Anne got back she had to sit with her, trying to quiet her till the Doctor came back. That wasn't till nearly two in the morning, when he reached home, dead beat, saying he'd come round the turnpike from the Riven Rock Road and seen no sign of either Sylvia or Jack Reddy.

No one at Mapleshade saw Sylvia leave the house, no one in Longwood saw her pass through the village, yet, two and a half hours from the time she had made the date with Mr Reddy, she was seen again, over a hundred miles from her home, in the last place anyone would have expected to find her.

Way up on the turnpike, two miles from Cresset's Crossing, there's a sort of roadhouse where the farm hands spend their evenings and automobilists stop for drinks and gasoline. It's got a shady reputation, being frequented by a rough class of people and once there was a dago – a laborer on Cresset's Farm – killed there in a drunken row. It's called the Wayside Arbor, which doesn't fit, sounding innocent and rural, though in the back there is a trellis with grapes growing over it and tables set out under it in warm weather.

At this season it's a dreary looking spot, an old frame cottage a few yards back from the road, with a broken-down piazza and a door painted green leading into the bar. Along the top of the piazza goes the sign "Wayside Arbor," with advertisements for some kind of beer at each end of it, and in the window there's more advertisements for whisky and crackers and soft drinks. Nailed to one of the piazza posts is a public telephone sign standing out very prominent.

At the time of the Hesketh mystery I'd only seen it once, one day in the summer when I was out in a hired car with Mrs Galway and two gentlemen friends from New York. We'd been to Bloomington by train and were motoring back and stopped to get some beer. But we ladies, not liking the looks of the place, wouldn't go in and had our beer brought out to us by the proprietor, Jake Hines, a tough-looking customer in a shirt without a collar and one of his suspenders broken.

It's very lonesome round there. The nearest house is Cresset's, a half mile away across the fields. Back of it and all round is Cresset's land, some of it planted in crops and then strips of woods, making the country in summer look lovely with the dark and the light green.

Sunday evening there were only two people in the Wayside Arbor bar, Hines and his servant, Tecla Rabine, a Bohemian woman. Mrs Hines was upstairs in the room above in bed with a cold. There was a fire burning in the stove, as a good many of Hines's customers were the dagoes that work at Cresset's and the other farms and they liked the place warm. Hines was reading the paper and Tecla Rabine was cleaning up the bar before she went upstairs, she having a toothache and wanting to get off to bed.

At the inquest Hines swore that he heard no sound of a car or of wheels – which, he said, he would have noticed, as that generally meant business – when there was a step on the piazza, the door opened and a lady came in. He didn't know who she was but saw right off she wasn't the kind that you'd expect to see in his place. She had on a long dark fur coat, a close-fitting plush hat with a Shetland veil pushed up round the brim, and looked pale, and, he thought, scared. It was Sylvia Hesketh, but he didn't know that till afterward.

She asked him right off if she could use his telephone and he pointed to the booth in the corner. She went in and closed the door and Hines stepped to the window and looked out to see if there was a car or a carriage that he hadn't heard, the mud making the road soft. But there was nothing there. Before he was through looking he heard the booth door open and turning back saw her come out. He said she wasn't five minutes sending her message.

That telephone message was the most mysterious one in the case. It was transmitted through the Corona Exchange to Firehill and there was no one in the world who heard it but Jack Reddy. I'm going to put it down here, copied from the newspaper reports of the inquest:

Oh, Jack, is that you? It's Sylvia. Thank Heavens you're there. I'm in trouble, I want you. I've done something dreadful. I'll tell you when I see you. I'll explain everything and you won't be angry. Come and get me – start now, this minute. Come up the Firehill Road to the Turnpike and I'll be there waiting, where the roads meet. Don't ask any questions now. When you hear you'll understand. And don't let anyone know – the servants or anyone. You've got to keep it quiet, it's vitally important, for my sake. Come, come quick.

That was all. Before he could ask her a question she'd disconnected. And, naturally, he made no effort to find out where the call had come from, being in such a hurry to get to her – Sylvia who was in trouble and wanted him to come.

When she came out of the booth she carried a small purse in her hand and Hines then noticed that she had only one glove on – the left – and that her right hand was scratched in several places. Thinking she looked cold he asked her if she would have something to drink and she said no, then pushed back her cuff and looked at a bracelet watch set in diamonds and sapphires that she wore on her wrist.

"Twenty minutes to ten," she said. "I'll wait here for a little while if you don't mind."

She went over to the stove, pulled up a chair and sat down, spreading her hands out to the heat, and when they were warm, opening her coat collar, and turning it back from her neck. Both Hines and Tecla Rabine noticed that her feet were muddy and that there were twigs and dead leaves caught in the edge of her skirt. As she didn't seem inclined to say anything, Hines, who admitted that he was ready to burst with curiosity, began to question her, trying to find out where she'd come from and what she was waiting for.

"You come a long way, I guess," he said.

She just nodded.

"From Bloomington maybe?" he asked.

"No, the other direction – toward Longwood."

"Car broken down?" he said next, and she answered sort of indifferent,

"Yes, it's down the road."

"Maybe I might go and lend a hand," he suggested and she answered quick to that:

"No, it's not necessary. They can fix it themselves," then she added, after a minute, "I've telephoned for someone to come for me and if the car's really broken we can tow it back."

That seemed so straight and natural that Hines began to get less curious, still he wanted to know who she was and tried to find out.

"You come a long ride if you come from Longwood," he said.

But he didn't get any satisfaction, for she answered:

"Is it a long way there?"

"About a hundred and eighteen miles by the turnpike – a good bit shorter by the Firehill Road, but that's pretty bad after these rains.

"Most of the roads *are* bad, I suppose," she said, as if she wasn't thinking of her words.

They were silent for a bit, then he tried again:

"What's broke in your auto?"

And she answered that sharp as if he annoyed her and she was setting him back in his place:

"My good man, I haven't the least idea. That's the chauffeur's business, not mine."

He asked her some more questions but he couldn't get anything out of her. He said she treated him sort of haughty as if she wanted him to stop. So after a while he said no more, but sat by the bar pretending to read his paper. Tecla Rabine came and went, tidying up for the night and none of them said a word.

A little before ten she got up and buttoned her coat, saying she was going. Hines was surprised and asked her if she wouldn't wait there for the auto, and she said no, she'd walk up the road and meet it.

He asked her which way it was coming and she said: "By the Firehill Road. How far is that from here?"

He told her about a quarter of a mile and she answered that she'd just about time to get there and catch it as it came into the turnpike.

Hines urged her to stay but she said no, she was cramped with sitting and needed a little walk; it was early yet and there was nothing to be afraid of. She bid him goodnight very cordial and pleasant and went out.

He stood in the doorway watching her as far as he could see, then told Tecla, whose toothache was bad, to go to bed. After she'd gone he locked up, went upstairs to his wife and told her about the strange lady. His wife said he'd done wrong to let her go, it wasn't right for a person like that to be alone on such a solitary road, especially with some of the farm hands, queer foreigners, no better than animals.

She worked upon his feelings till she got him nervous and he was going to get a lantern and start out when he heard the sound of an auto horn in the distance. He stepped to the window and watched and presently saw a big car with one lamp dark coming at a great clip down from the Firehill Road direction. The moon had come out a short while before, so that if he'd looked he could have seen the people in the car, but supposing it was the one the lady was waiting for, he turned from the window, and, thinking no more about it, went to bed.

Before he was off to sleep he heard another auto horn and the whirr of a car passing. He couldn't say how long after this was, as he was half asleep.

How long he'd slept he didn't know – it really was between four and five in the morning – when he was roused by a great battering at the door and a sound of voices. He jumped up just as he was, ran to the window and opened it. There in the road he could see plain – the clouds were gone, the moon sailing clear and high – a motor and some people all talking very excited, and one voice, a woman's, saying over and over, "Oh, how horrible – how horrible!"

He took them for a party of merry-makers, half drunk and wanting more, and called down fierce and savage:

"What in thunder are you doing there?"

One of them, a man standing on the steps of the piazza, looked up at him and said:

"There's a murdered woman up the road here, that's all."

As he ran to the place with the men – there were two of them – they told him how they were on a motor trip with their wives and that night were going from Bloomington to Huntley. The moon being so fine they were going slow, otherwise they never would have found the body, which was lying by the roadside. A pile of brushwood had been thrown over it, but one hand had fallen out beyond the branches and one of the women had seen it, white in the moonlight.

They had unfastened an auto lamp and it was standing on the ground beside her. Hines lifted it and looked at her. She lay partly on her side, her coat loosely drawn round her. The right arm was flung out as if when the body stiffened it might have slipped down from a position across the chest. As he held the lantern close he saw below the hat, pulled down on her head, with the torn rags of veil still clinging to it, a thin line of blood running down to where the pearl necklace rested, untouched, round her throat.

It was Sylvia Hesketh, her skull fractured by a blow that had cracked her head like an egg shell.

V

There were so many puzzling "leads" and so much that was inexplicable and mysterious in the Hesketh case that it'll be easier to follow if, in this chapter, I put down what the other people, who were either suspects or important witnesses, did on that Sunday.

Some of it may not be interesting, but it's necessary to know if you're going to get a clear understanding of a case that baffled the police and pretty nearly.... There I go again. But it's awfully hard when you're not used to it to keep things in their right order.

I've told how Jim Donahue said he put Sylvia on the train for the Junction that night at seven-thirty. Both Jim and the ticket agent said they'd seen her and Jim had spoken to her. She carried a hand bag, wore a long dark fur coat and a small close-fitting hat that showed her hair. Both men also noticed in her hand the gold mesh purse with a diamond monogram that she always carried. Over her face was tied a black figured veil that hid her features, but there was no mistaking the hair, the voice, or the gold mesh purse.

Sands, the Pullman conductor, said this same woman rode down in his train to the Junction, where she got off. Clark, the station agent at the Junction, saw her step from the car to the platform. After that he lost track of her as he was busy with the branch line train which left at eight-forty-five and was the last one up that night. No woman went on it, there were only two passengers, both men.

The Doctor didn't make his whole story public till the inquest. They said afterward the police knew it, but it was his policy to say little and keep quiet in Mapleshade. What we in the village did know – partly from the papers, partly from people – was that after the message from Mrs Fowler saying Sylvia had eloped, he told Mrs Dalzell he would have to leave, having been called away to an important case. When the Dalzells' chauffeur brought his car round he asked the man several questions about the shortest way to get to the turnpike. The chauffeur told him that the best traveling would be by the Riven Rock Road, which he would have to go to the Junction to get. The Doctor left the Dalzells' at a little after eight, alone in his car.

He reached the Junction about eight-thirty-five, a few minutes after the train from Longwood had arrived. On the platform he spoke to Clark, asking him how to get to the Riven Rock Road. Clark gave him the directions, then saw him disappear round the station building. Neither Clark nor anyone at the Junction – there were very few there at that hour – saw him leave in his car, though they heard the honk of the auto horn.

But it was Jack Reddy's movements that everybody was most interested in. There was no secret about them.

Sunday at lunch he told Gilsey that he was going away for a trip for a few days. If he stayed longer than he expected he'd wire back for his things, but, as it was, he'd only want his small auto trunk, which he'd take with him. When Mrs Gilsey was packing this he joked her about having a good time while he was gone, and she told him that, as there'd be no dinner that night, she and Gilsey'd go over to a neighbor's, take supper there and spend the evening. After that he asked Casey, the chauffeur, to have the racing car brought round at five, to see that the tank was full, a footwarmer in it and the heaviest rugs and a drum of gasoline, as he was going on a long trip.

At five he left Firehill in the racer. At a quarter to seven two boys saw him pass the Longwood Station in the direction of Maple Lane. He said he came back through the outskirts of the village at seven-thirty, but no one could be found who had seen him.

After he left Firehill the Gilseys cleared up and walked across the fields to the Jaycocks' farm, where they spent the evening, coming home at ten and finding the house dark and quiet. Casey went to another neighbor's, where he stayed till midnight, playing cards.

He slept over the garage, and about four in the morning – he looked at his watch afterward – was awakened by a sound down below in the garage. He listened and made sure that someone was trying to roll the doors back very slow and with as little noise as possible. Casey's a bold, nervy boy, and he reached for his revolver and crept barefooted to the head of the stairs. On the top step he stooped down and looked through the banisters, and saw against the big square of the open doors a man standing, with a car behind him shining in the moonlight.

He thought it was a burglar, so, with his revolver up and ready, he called:

"Hello, there. What are you doing?"

The man gave a great start, and then he heard Mr Reddy's voice:

"Oh, Casey, did I wake you? I've come back unexpectedly. Help me get this car in."

They ran the car in, and, when Casey went to tell how he thought it was a burglar and was going to shoot, he noticed that Mr Reddy hardly listened to him, but was gruff and short. All he said was that he'd changed his mind about the trip, and then unstrapped his trunk from the back and turned to go. In the doorway he stopped as if he'd had a sudden thought, and said over his shoulder:

"You don't want to mention this in Longwood. I'm getting a little sick of the gossip there over my affairs."

Casey went back to bed and in the morning, when he looked at the car, found it was caked with mud, even the wind-guard spattered. At seven he crossed over to the house for his breakfast and told the Gilseys that Mr Reddy was back. They were surprised, but decided, as he'd been out so late, they'd not disturb him till he rang for his breakfast.

Monday morning was clear and sharp, the first real frost of the season. All the time I was dressing I was thinking about the elopement and how queer it was Mrs Fowler saying they'd gone by turnpike and Jim Donahue saying he'd seen Sylvia leave on the train. I worked it out that they'd made some change of plans at the last moment. But the *way* they'd eloped didn't matter to me. Small things like that didn't cut any ice when I was all tormented wondering if it was for the best that my hero should marry a wild girl who no one could control.

I hadn't been long at the switchboard, and was sitting sideways in my chair looking out of the window when I saw Dr Fowler's auto drive up with the Doctor and a strange man in it. I twirled round quick and was the business-like operator. I'll bet no one would have thought that the girl sitting so calm and indifferent in that swivel chair was just boiling with excitement and curiosity.

The Doctor looked bad, yellow as wax, with his eyes sunk and inflamed. He didn't take any notice of me beside a fierce sort of look and a gruff,

"Give me Corona 1-4-2."

That was Firehill. I jacked in and the Doctor went into the booth and shut the door. The strange man stood with his hands behind him, looking out of the window. I didn't know then that he was a detective, and I don't think anyone ever would have guessed it. If you'd asked me I'd have said he looked more like a clerk at the ribbon counter. But that's what he was, Walter Mills by name, engaged that morning, as we afterward knew, by the Doctor.

Watching him with one eye I leaned forward very cautiously, lifted up the cam and listened in on the conversation:

"Is this Gilsey?"

Then Gilsey's nice old voice, "Yes, sir. Who is it?"

The Doctor's was quick and hard:

"Never mind that – it doesn't matter. Do you happen to know where Mr Reddy is?"

My heart gave a big jump – he hadn't caught them! They'd got away and been married!

"Yes, sir, Mr Reddy's here."

There was just a minute's pause before the Doctor answered. In that minute all sorts of ideas went flashing through my head the way they say you see things before you drown. Then came the Doctor's voice with a curious sort of quietness in it.

"*There*, at Firehill?"

"Yes, sir. Can I take any message? Mr Reddy was out very late last night and isn't up yet."

The Doctor answered that very cordially, all the hurry and hardness gone.

"Oh, that's all right. I'll not disturb him. No, I won't bother with a message. I'll call up later. Thanks very much. Goodbye."

I dropped back in my chair, tapping with a pencil on the corner of the drawer and looking sideways at the Doctor as he came out of the booth. He had a queer look, his eyes keen and bright, and there was some color in his face. The strange man turned round, and the Doctor gave him a glance sharp as a razor, but all he said was: "Come on, Mills," and they went out and mounted into the car.

When the door banged on them I drew a deep breath and flattened out against the chair back. They *hadn't* eloped!

Gee, it was a relief! Not because of myself. Honest to God, that's straight. I knew I couldn't have him any more than I could have had the Kohinoor diamond. It was because I *knew* –

deep down where you feel the truth – that Sylvia Hesketh wasn't the girl for him to marry.

That was about half-past eight. It was after ten when a message came for Mapleshade that made the world turn upside down and left me white and sick. It was from the Coroner and said that Sylvia Hesketh had been found that morning on the turnpike, murdered.

Poor Mrs Fowler took it!

Anne Hennessey told me afterward that she heard her scream on the other side of the house. I heard it, too, and it raised *my* hair – and then a lot of words coming thin and shrill along the wire. "Sylvia, my daughter – dead – murdered?" It was awful, I hate to think of it.

Nora and Anne ran at the sound and found Mrs Fowler all wild and screaming, with the receiver hanging down. I could hear them, a babble of tiny little voices as if I had a line on some part of Purgatory where the spirits were crying and wailing.

Suddenly it stopped – somebody had hung up. I waited, shaking there like a leaf and feeling like I'd a blow in the stomach. Then Mapleshade called and I heard Anne's voice, distinct but broken as if she'd been running.

"Molly, is that you? Do you by any chance know if the Doctor's in the village?"

"He was here a little while ago with a man calling up Firehill. Anne, I heard – it can't be true."

"Oh, it is – it is – I can't talk now. I've *got* to find him. Give me Firehill. He may have gone there. Quick, for God's sake!"

I gave it and heard her tell a man at the other end of the line.

I'll go on from here and tell what happened at Firehill. I've pieced it out from the testimony at the inquest and from what the Gilseys afterward told in the village.

The Doctor and Mills went straight out there from the Exchange. When they arrived Gilsey told him Mr Reddy wasn't up yet, but he'd call him. The Doctor, however, said the matter was urgent and they couldn't lose a minute, so the three of them went upstairs together and Gilsey knocked at the door. After he'd knocked twice a sleepy voice called out, "Come in," and Gilsey opened the door.

It led into a sitting-room with a bedroom opening off it. On a sofa just opposite the door was Jack Reddy, dressed and stretched out as if he'd been asleep.

At first he saw no one but Gilsey and sat up with a start, saying sharply:

"What's the matter? Does anyone want me?"

Gilsey said, "Yes, two gentlemen to see you," and stepped to one side to let the Doctor and Mills enter.

When Reddy saw the Doctor he jumped to his feet and stood looking at him. He didn't say "Good morning" or any sort of greeting, but was silent, as if he was holding himself still, waiting to hear what the Doctor was going to say.

He hadn't to wait long. The Doctor, in the doorway, went right to the point.

"Mr Reddy," said he, "where's my daughter?"

Reddy answered in a quiet, composed voice:

"I don't know, Dr Fowler."

"You do!" shouted the Doctor. "You ran away with her last night. What have you done with her?"

Reddy said in the same dignified way:

"I haven't done anything. I know nothing about her. I haven't any more idea than you where she is."

At that the Doctor got beside himself. He shouted out furiously:

"You have, you d—d liar, and I'll get it out of you," and he made a lunge at Reddy to seize him. But Mills jumped in and grabbed his arm. Holding it he said, trying to quiet down the Doctor:

"Just wait a minute, Dr Fowler. Maybe when Mr Reddy sees that we understand the situation, he'll be willing to explain."

Then he turned to Reddy: "There's no good prevaricating. Your letter to Miss Hesketh has been found. Now we're all agreed that we don't want any talk or scandal about this. If you want to get out of the affair without trouble to yourself and others you'd better tell the truth. Where is she?"

"Who the devil are you?" Reddy cried out suddenly, as mad as the Doctor, and before Mills could answer, the branch telephone on the desk rang.

Reddy gave a loud exclamation and made a jump for it. But Mills got before him and caught him. He struggled to get away till the Doctor seized him on the other side. They fought for a moment, and then got him back against the door, all the time the telephone ringing like mad. As they wrestled with him Mills called over his shoulder to Gilsey:

"Answer that telephone, quick."

Gilsey, scared most out of his wits, ran to the phone and took down the receiver. Anne Hennessey was at the other end with her awful message.

When he got it Gilsey gave a cry like he was stabbed, and turned to Mr Reddy, pinioned against the door.

"Good Lord, have mercy, Mr Jack," he gasped out. "Miss Hesketh's dead. She's murdered – on the turnpike – murdered last night!"

The Doctor dropped Reddy, tore the instrument out of Gilsey's hand and took the rest of the message.

Reddy turned the color of ashes. There wasn't any need to hold him. He fell back against the door with his jaw dropped and his eyes staring like a man in a trance. Gilsey thought he was going to die and was for running to him, crying out, "Oh, Mr Jack, don't look that way." But Mills caught the old servant by the arm and held him back, watching Reddy as sharp as a ferret.

The Doctor turned from the phone and said: "It's true. Miss Hesketh's been murdered."

There was a dead silence. The click of the receiver falling into its hook was the only sound. The three other men – the Doctor as white as death, too – stood staring at Reddy. And then, seeing those three faces, he burst out like he was crazy:

"No – she's not – she can't be! I was there; I went the moment I got her message. I was on the turnpike where she said she'd be. I was up and down there most of the night. And – and—" he stopped suddenly and put his hands over his face, groaning, "Oh, my God, Sylvia – why didn't you tell me?"

He lurched forward and dropped into a chair, his hands over his face, moaning like an animal in pain.

VI

Longwood was stunned. By noon everybody knew it and there was no more business that day. The people stood in groups, talking in whispers as if they were at a funeral. And in the afternoon it *was* like a funeral, the body coming back by train and being taken from the depot to Mapleshade in one of the Doctor's farm wagons. It lay under a sheet and as the wagon passed through the crowd you couldn't hear a sound, except for a woman crying here and there.

Then it was as if a spring that held the people dumb and still was loosed and the excitement burst up. I never saw anything like it. It seemed like every village up and down the line had emptied itself into Longwood. Farmers and laborers and loafers swarmed along the streets, the rich came in motors, tearing to Mapleshade, and the police were everywhere, as if they'd sprung out of the ground.

By afternoon the reporters came pouring in from town. The Inn was full up with them and they were buzzing round my exchange like flies. Some of them tried to get hold of me and that night had the nerve to come knocking at Mrs Galway's side door, demanding the telephone girl. But, believe me, I sat tight and said nothing – nothing to them. The police were after me mighty quick, and there was a séance over Corwin's Drug Store when I felt like I was being put to the third degree. I told them all I knew, job or no job, for I guessed right off that that talk

I'd overheard on the phone might be an important clew. They kept it close. It wasn't till after the inquest that the press got it.

Before the inquest every sort of rumor was flying about, and the papers were full of crazy stories, not half of them true. I'd read about places and people I knew as well as my own face in the mirror, and they'd sound like a dime novel, so colored up and twisted round the oldest inhabitant wouldn't have recognized them.

To get at the facts was a job, but, knowing who was reliable and who wasn't, I questioned and ferreted and, I guess, before I was done I had them pretty straight.

Sylvia had been killed by a blow on the side of her head – a terrible blow. A sheriff's deputy I know told me that in all his experience he had seen nothing worse. Her hat had evidently shielded the scalp. It was pulled well down over her head, the long pin bent but still thrust through it. Where she had been hit the plush was torn but not the thick interlining, and her hair, all loosened, was hanging down against her neck. There was a wound – not deep, more like a tearing of the skin, on the lower part of her cheek. It was agreed that she had been struck only once by some heavy implement that had a sharp or jagged edge. Though the woods and fields had been thoroughly searched nothing had been discovered that could have dealt the blow. Whatever he had used the murderer had either successfully hidden it or taken it away with him. The deputy told me it looked to him as if it might have been some farming tool like a spade, or even a heavy branch broken from a tree. The way the body was arranged, the coat drawn smoothly together, the branches completely covering her, showed that the murderer had taken time to conceal his crime, though why he had not drawn the body back into the thick growth of bushes was a point that puzzled everybody.

It was impossible to trace any footprints, as the automobile party and Hines had trodden the earth about her into a muddy mass, and the grass along the edge was too thick and springy to hold any impression.

Close behind the place where she lay twigs of the screening trees were snapped and bent as if her assailant had broken through them.

There were people who said Hines would have been arrested on the spot if robbery had been added to murder. But the jewelry was all on her, more than he said he had noticed when she was in the Wayside Arbor. The pearl necklace alone was worth twenty thousand dollars, and just below it, clasping her gown over the chest, was a diamond cross, an old ornament of her mother's, made of the finest Brazilian stones. In the pocket of her coat was a purse with forty-eight dollars in it. So right at the start the theory of robbery was abandoned.

Another inexplicable thing was the disappearance of the French maid, Virginia Dupont. Jack Reddy denied any knowledge of her. He said Sylvia had never mentioned bringing her with them and he didn't think intended to do so. The Mapleshade people thought differently, all declaring that Sylvia depended on her and took her wherever she went. One of the mysteries about the woman that was quickly cleared up was the walk she had taken to the village on Sunday morning. This was to meet Mr Reddy and take from him the letter for Sylvia which had been found in the desk.

I know from what I heard that the police were keen to find her, but she had dropped out of sight without leaving a trace. No one at Mapleshade knew anything about her or her connections. She was not liked in the house or the village and had made no friends. On her free Sundays she'd go to town and when she returned say very little about where she'd been. A search of her rooms showed nothing, except that she seemed to have left her clothes behind her. She was last seen at Mapleshade by Nora Magee, who, at half-past five on Sunday, met her on the third floor stairs. Nora was off for a walk to the village with Harper and was in a hurry. She asked Virginie if she was going out and Virginie said no, she felt sick and was going up to lie down till she'd be wanted to help Miss Sylvia dress for dinner.

If you ask me was anyone suspected at this stage I'd answer "yes," but people were afraid to say who. There was talk about Hines on the street and in the postoffice, but it was only when you were close shut in your own room or walking quiet up a side street that the person with you would whisper the Doctor's name. Nobody dared say it aloud, but there wasn't a soul in Longwood who didn't know about the quarreling at Mapleshade, whose was the money that ran it, and the will that left everything to Mrs Fowler if her daughter died.

But no arrests were made. Everything was waiting on the inquest, and we all heard that there were important facts – already known to the police – which would not be made public till then.

Wednesday afternoon they held the inquest at Mapleshade. The authorities had rounded up a bunch of witnesses, I among them. The work in the Exchange had piled up so we'd had to send a hurry call for help to headquarters and I left the office in charge of a new girl, Katie Reilly, Irish, a tall, gawky thing, who was going to work with us hereafter on split hours.

Going down Maple Lane it was like a target club outing or a political picnic, except for the solemn faces. I saw Hines and his party, and the railway men, and a lot of queer guys that I took to be the jury. Halfway there a gang of reporters passed me, talking loud, and swinging along in their big overcoats. Near the black pine the toot of a horn made me stand back and Jack Reddy's roadster scudded by, he driving, with Casey beside him, and the two old Gilseys, pale and peaked in the back seat.

They held the inquest in the dining-room, with the coroner sitting at one end of the long shiny table and the jury grouped round the other. Take it from me, it was a gloomy sight. The day outside was cold and cloudy, and through the French windows that looked out on the lawns, the light came still and gray, making the faces look paler than they already were. It was a grand, beautiful room with a carved stone fireplace where logs were burning. Back against the walls were sideboards with silver dishes on them and hand-painted portraits hung on the walls.

But the thing you couldn't help looking at – and that made all the splendor just nothing – were Sylvia's clothes hanging over the back of a chair, and on a little table near them her hat and veil, the one glove she had had on, and the heap of jewelry. All those fine garments and the precious stones worth a fortune seemed so pitiful and useless now.

We were awful silent at first, a crowd of people sitting along the walls, staring straight ahead or looking on the ground. Now and then someone would move uneasily and make a rustle, but there were moments so still you could hear the fire snapping and the scratching of the reporters' pencils. They were just behind me, bunched up at a table in front of the window. When the Doctor came in everyone was as quiet as death and the eyes on him were like the eyes of images, so fixed and steady. Mrs Fowler was not present – they sent for her later – but Nora and Anne were there as pale as ghosts.

The Coroner opened up by telling about how and where the deceased had been found, the position, the surroundings, etc., etc., and then called Dr Graham, who was the county physician and had made the autopsy.

A good deal of what he said I didn't understand – it was to prove that death resulted from a fracture of the skull. He could not state the exact hour of dissolution, but said it was in the earlier part of the night, some time before twelve. He described the condition of the scalp which had been partially protected by the hat, thick as it was with a plush outside and a heavy interlining. This was held up and then given to the jury to examine. I saw it plainly as they passed it from hand to hand – a small dark automobile hat, with a tear in one side and some shreds of black Shetland veil hanging to its edge. She bore no other marks of violence save a few small scratches on her right hand. She had evidently been attacked unexpectedly and had had no time to fight or struggle.

The automobilists who had found the body came next. Only the men were present – two nice-looking gentlemen – the ladies having been excused. They told what I have already written, one of them making the creeps go down your spine, describing how his wife said she saw the hand in the moonlight, and how he walked back, laughing, and pulled off the brushwood.

After that Mrs Fowler came, all swathed up in black and looking like a haggard old woman. The Coroner spoke very kind to her. When she got to the quarrel between Sylvia and the Doctor her voice began to tremble and she could hardly go on. It was pitiful to see but she had to tell it, and about the other quarrels too. Then she pulled herself together and told about going up to Sylvia's room and finding the letter.

The Coroner stopped her there and taking a folded paper from the table beside him said it was the letter and read it out to us. It was dated Firehill, Nov. 21st.

" DEAREST:

"All right. This evening at seven by the pine. We'll go in my racer to Bloomington and be married there by Fiske, the man I told you about. It'll be a long ride but at the end we'll find happiness waiting for us. Don't disappoint me – don't do what you did the other time. Believe in my love and trust yourself to me – JACK."

In the silence that followed you could hear the fire falling together with a little soft rustle. All the eyes turned as if they were on pivots and looked at Jack Reddy – all but mine. I kept them on Mrs Fowler and never moved them till she was led, bent and sobbing, out of the room.

Nora Magee was the next, and I heard them say afterward made a good witness. The coroner asked her – and Anne when her turn came – very particular about the jewelry, what was gone, how many pieces and such questions. And then it came out that nobody – not even Mrs Fowler – knew exactly what Sylvia had. She was all the time buying new ornaments or having her old ones reset and the only person who kept track of her possessions was Virginie Dupont. All any of them could be sure of was that the jewel box was empty, and the toilet articles, fitted bag, and gold mesh purse were gone.

Hines was called after that. He was all slicked up in his store clothes and looked very different to what he had that day in the summer. Though anyone could see he was scared blue, the perspiration on his forehead and his big, knotty hands twiddling at his tie and his watch chain; he told his story very clear and straightforward. I think everyone was impressed by it and by Mrs Hines, who followed him. She was a miserable looking little rat of a woman, with inflamed eyes and a long drooping nose, but she corroborated all he said, and – anyway, to me – it sounded true.

Tecla Rabine, the Bohemian servant, followed, and when she walked over to sit in the chair, keyed up as I was, I came near laughing. She was a large, fat woman with a goodhumored red face and little twinkling eyes, and she sure was a sight, bulging out of a black cloth suit that was the fashion when Columbus landed. On her head was a fancy straw hat with one mangy feather sticking straight up at the back, and the last touch was her face, one side still swollen out from her toothache, and looking for all the world as if she had a quid in her cheek.

Though she spoke in a queer, foreign dialect, she gave her testimony very well and she told something that no one – I don't think even the police – had heard before.

While Hines was locking up she went to her room but couldn't sleep because of the pain of her toothache.

"Ach," she said, spreading her hand out near her cheek, "it was out so far – swole out, and, oh, my God – *pain*!"

"Never mind your toothache," said the Coroner – "keep to the subject."

"How do I hear noises if my toothache doesn't make me to wake?" she asked, giving him a sort of indignant look.

Somebody laughed, a kind of choked giggle, and I heard one of those fresh write-up chaps behind me whisper:

"This is the comic relief."

"Oh, you heard noises – what kind of noises?"

"The scream," she said.

"You heard a scream?"

"Yes – one scream – far away, up toward Cresset's Crossing. I go crazy with the pain and after Mr Hines is come upstairs I go down to the kitchen to make—" she stopped, looking up in the air – "what you call him?" – she put her hand flat on the side of her face – "for here, to stop the pain."

"Do you mean a poultice?"

She grinned all over and nodded.

"Yes, that's him. I make hot water on the gas, and then, way off, I hear a scream."

"What time was that?"

"The kitchen clock says ten minutes past ten."

"What did you do?"

She looked surprised.

"I make the – you know the name – for my ache."

"Didn't you go out and investigate – even go to the door?"

She shook her head and gave a sort of good-humored laugh as if she was explaining things to a child.

"Go out. For why? If I go out for screams I go out when the dagoes fight, and when the automobiles be pass – up and down all night, often drunken and making noises;" she shrugged her shoulders sort of careless; "I no be bothered with screams."

"Did you go to bed?"

"I do. I make the medicine for my swole up face and go upstairs."

"Did you hear any more screams?"

"No – there are no more. If there are I would have hear them, for I can't sleep ever all night. All I hear is automobiles – many automobiles passing up and down and maybe – two, three, four times – the horns sounding."

The Coroner asked her a few more questions, principally about Hines' movements, and her answers, if you could get over the lingo, were all clear and in line with what Hines had said.

The railway men followed her, Sands and Clark and Jim Donahue. Jim was as nervous as a cat, holding his hat in his hands and twisting it round like a plate he was drying. He told about the woman he put on the seven-thirty train on Sunday night.

"Where did you first see this woman?" he was asked.

"On the platform, just before the train came in. She came down along it, out of the dark."

"Can you swear it was Miss Hesketh?"

Jim didn't think he could swear because he couldn't see her face plain, it being covered with a figured black veil. But he never thought of it being anyone else.

"Why did you think it was she?"

"Because it looked like her. It was her coat and her gold purse and I'd know her hair anywhere. And when I spoke to her and said: 'Goodevening, Miss Hesketh, going to leave us?' it was her voice that answered: 'Yes, Jim, I'm going away for a few days.'"

"Did you have any more conversation with her?"

"No, because the train came along then. She got in and I handed her her bag and said 'Goodnight.'"

When he was asked to describe the bag, he said he hadn't noticed it except that it was a medium sized bag, he thought, dark colored.

Then he was shown the clothes – that was heart-rending. The Coroner held them up, the long fur coat, the little plush hat, and the one glove. He thought they were the same but it was hard to tell, the platform being so dark – anyway, it was them sort of clothes the lady had on, and though he couldn't be sure of the glove he had noticed that her gloves were light colored.

Sands, the Pullman conductor, and Clark, from the Junction, testified that they'd seen the same woman on the train and at the Junction. Sands particularly noticed the gold mesh purse because she took her ticket out of it. He addressed her as Miss Hesketh and she had answered him, but only to say "Good evening."

Then came the Firehill servants. The two old Gilseys were dreadfully upset. Mrs Gilsey cried and poor old David kept hesitating and looking at Mr Reddy, but the stamp of truth was on every word they said. Casey followed them, telling what I've already written.

When Mr Reddy was called a sort of stir went over the people. Everybody was curious to hear his story, as we'd only got bits of it, most of them wild rumors. And there wasn't a soul in Longwood that didn't grieve for him, plunged down at the moment when he thought he was most happy into such an awful tragedy. As he sat down in the chair opposite the Coroner, the room was as still as a tomb, even the reporters behind me not making so much as the scratch of a pen.

He looked gray and pinched, his eyes burnt out like a person's who hasn't slept for nights. You could see he was nervous, for he kept crossing and uncrossing his knees, and he didn't give his evidence nearly so clear and continued as the newspapers had it. He'd stop every now and then as if he didn't remember or as if he was thinking of the best way to express himself.

He began by telling how he and Sylvia had arranged to go in his car to Bloomington, and there be married by his friend Fiske, an Episcopal clergyman. The Coroner asked him if Fiske expected them and he said no, he hadn't had time to let him know as the elopement was decided on hurriedly.

"Why was the decision hurried?" the Coroner asked and he answered low, as if he was reluctant to say it.

"Because Miss Hesketh had a violent quarrel with her stepfather on Saturday morning. It was not till after that that she made up her mind she would go with me."

"Did you know at the time what that quarrel was about?"

His face got a dull red and he said low.

"Yes, she told me of it in a letter she wrote me immediately afterward."

Then he told how on Saturday night he had received a special delivery letter from her, telling of the quarrel and agreeing to the elopement. That letter he had destroyed. He answered it the next morning, she having directed him to bring it in himself and deliver it to Virginie, who would meet him opposite Corwin's drugstore. This he did, the letter being the one already in evidence.

The Coroner asked him to explain the sentence which said "Don't disappoint me – don't do what you did the other time." He looked straight in front of him and answered:

"We had made a plan to elope once before and she had backed out."

"Do you know why?"

"It was too – too unusual – too unconventional. When it came to the scandal of an elopement she hung back."

"Is it your opinion that the quarrel with Dr Fowler made her agree the second time?"

"I know nothing about that."

Then he told of leaving Firehill, coming into Longwood, and going down Maple Lane.

"I reached there a few minutes before seven and ran down to the pine tree where I was to meet her. I drew up to one side of the road and waited. During the time I waited – half an hour – I neither saw nor heard anybody. At half-past seven I decided she had changed her mind again and left."

"You didn't go to the house?"

"No – I was not welcome at the house. She had told me not to go there."

"You were in the habit of seeing her somewhere else, though?"

His face got red again and you could see he had to make an effort not to get angry.

"After I had heard from Miss Hesketh and seen from Dr Fowler's manner that I was not wanted at Mapleshade, I saw her at intervals. Once or twice we went for walks in the woods, and a few times, perhaps three or four, I met her on the turnpike and took her for a drive in my car."

He then went on to tell how he drove back to Firehill, reaching there a little after nine. The place was empty and he went up to his room. He didn't know how long he'd been there when the telephone rang. It was the mysterious message from her.

He repeated it slowly, evidently trying to give it word for word. You could have heard a pin drop when he ended.

"Did you attempt to question her on the phone?"

"No, it all went too quick and I was too astonished."

"Did you get the impression that she was in any grave danger?"

"No, I never thought of that. She was very rash and impulsive and I thought she'd done some foolhardy thing and had turned to me as the one person on whom she could rely."

"What do you mean by foolhardy?"

He gave a shrug and threw out his hands.

"The sort of thing a child might do – some silly, thoughtless action. She was full of spirit and daring; you never could be sure of what she mightn't try. I didn't think of any definite thing. I ran to the garage and got out my car and went northward up the Firehill Road. It was terrible traveling, and I should say it took me nearly three-quarters of an hour to make the distance. When I was nearing the pike I sounded my horn to let her know I was coming.

"Just before I got there the clouds had broken and the moon come out. The whole landscape was flooded with light, and I made no doubt I'd see her as soon as I turned into the pike. But she wasn't there. I slowed up and waited, looking up and down, for I'd no idea which way she was coming, but there wasn't a sign of her. As far as I could see, the road was lifeless and deserted. Then I ran up and down – a mile or two either way – but there was no one to be seen."

"Did you hear any sounds in the underbrush – footsteps, breaking of twigs?"

"I heard nothing. The place was as still as the grave. I made longer runs up and down, looking along both sides and now and then waiting and sounding the auto horn."

"Did you stop at any of the farms or cottages and make inquiries?"

"No. I didn't do that because I had no thought of her being in any real danger and because she'd cautioned me against letting anyone know. After I'd searched the main road thoroughly for several miles and gone up several branch roads I began to think she'd played a joke on me."

"Do you mean fooled you?"

"Yes – the whole thing began to look that way. Her not being at the rendezvous in Maple Lane and then phoning me to meet her at a place, which, when I came to think of it, it was nearly impossible for her to reach in that space of time. It seemed the only reasonable explanation – and it was the sort of thing she might do. When I got the idea in my head it grew and," he looked down on the floor, his voice dropping low as if it was hard for him to speak, "I got blazing mad."

For a moment it seemed like he couldn't go on. In that moment I thought of how he must be feeling, remembering his rage against her while all the time she was lying cold and dead by the road.

"I was too angry to go home," he went on, "and not thinking much what I did, I let the car out and went up and down – I don't know how far – I don't remember – miles and miles."

"According to Mr Casey it was half-past four when you came back to the garage."

"I daresay; I didn't notice the time."

"You were from 9:30 to 4:30 on the road?"

"Yes."

"You spent those seven hours going up and down the turnpike and the intersecting roads?"

"Yes, but at first I waited – for half hours at a time in different places."

He looked straight at the Coroner as he said that, a deep steady look, more quiet and intent than he'd done since he started. I think it would have seemed to most people as if he was telling the absolute truth and wanted to impress it. But when a girl feels about a man as I did about him, she can see below the surface, and there was something about the expression of his face, about the tone of his voice, that made me think for the first time he was holding something back.

Then he went on and told about going home and falling asleep on the sofa, and about the doctor and Mills coming.

"When I saw the Doctor my first thought was that I must keep quiet till I found out what had happened. When he asked me where his daughter was I was startled as I realized she wasn't at home. But, even then, I hadn't any idea of serious trouble and I was determined to hold my tongue till I knew more than I did.

"The ring of the telephone gave me a shock. I had been expecting to get a call from her and instinctively I gave a jump for it. By that time I was sure she'd got into some silly scrape and

I wasn't going to have her stepfather finding out and starting another quarrel. They," he nodded his head at the Doctor and Mills, "caught on at once and made a rush for me.

"After that—" he lifted his hands and let them drop on his knees – "it was just as they've said. I was paralyzed. I don't know what I said. I only felt she'd been in danger and called on me and I'd failed her. I think for a few moments I was crazy."

His voice got so husky he could hardly speak and he bent his head down, looking at his hands. I guess every face in the room was turned to him but mine. I couldn't look at him but sat like a dummy, picking at my gloves, and inside, in my heart, I felt like I was crying. In the silence I heard one of the reporters whisper:

"Gee – poor chap! that's tough!"

He was asked some more questions, principally about what Sylvia had told him of the quarrels with her stepfather. You could see he was careful in his answers. According to what he said she'd only alluded to them in a general way as making the life at Mapleshade very uncomfortable.

He was just getting up when I saw one of the jurors pass a slip of paper across the table to the Coroner. He looked at it, then, as Mr Reddy was moving away, asked him to wait a minute; there was another question – had he stopped anywhere during Sunday night to get gasoline for his car?

Mr Reddy turned back and said very simply:

"No, I had an extra drum in the car."

"You used that?"

"Yes."

"What did you do with the drum?"

"Threw it into the bushes somewhere along the road."

"Do you know the place?"

He gave a sort of smile and shook his head.

"No, I don't remember. I don't know where I filled the tank. When it was done I pitched the drum back into the trees – somewhere along the turnpike."

Several more of us came after that, I among them. But the real sensation of the day was the Doctor's evidence, which I'll keep for the next chapter.

VII

The Doctor was as calm and matter-of-fact as if he were giving a lecture to a class of students. He looked much better than he did that morning in the Exchange; rested and with a good color. As he settled himself in the chair, I heard one of the reporters whisper:

"I wouldn't call that the mug of a murderer."

I looked over my shoulder right at the one who had spoken, a young chap with a round, rosy, innocent sort of face like a kid's and yellow hair standing up over his head as thick as sheep's wool. I'd seen him several times in the Exchange and knew his name was Babbitts and that the other fellows called him "Soapy." When he caught my eye he winked, and you couldn't be mad because it was like a big pink baby winking at you.

The Doctor told his story more straight and continuous than any of the others. It went along so clear from point to point, that the coroner didn't have to ask so many questions, and when he did the doctor was always ready with his answer. It sounded to me as if he'd thought out every detail, worked it up just right to get the best effect. He began with Saturday morning, when he'd got the call to go to the Dalzells'.

"An operation was performed early that afternoon and I stayed during the night and all the next day, going out on Sunday morning at ten for an hour's ride in my motor. I had decided to remain Sunday night too – though the patient was out of danger – when at about eight I received a telephone message from my wife saying Miss Hesketh had run away with Jack Reddy. Hearing from her that their route would be by the turnpike to Bloomington I made up my mind that my best course was to strike the turnpike and intercept them."

"You disapproved of their marriage?"

"Decidedly. Miss Hesketh was too young to know her own mind. Mr Reddy was not the husband I would have chosen for her – not to mention the distress it would have caused Mrs Fowler to have her daughter marry in that manner. My desire to keep the escapade secret made me tell Mrs Dalzell a falsehood – that I was called away on an important case.

"The Dalzells' chauffeur told me that the road from their place to the turnpike was impassable for motors. The best route for me would be to go to the Junction, where I could strike the Riven Rock Road, which came out on the turnpike about a mile from Cresset's Crossing. I had plenty of time, as the distance young Reddy would have to travel before he reached that point was nearly a hundred and twenty miles.

"I arrived at the Junction as the train for Philadelphia was drawing out. I spoke to Clark, the station agent, about the road, and, after getting the directions, walked round the depot to the back platform, where my car stood. As I passed the door of the waiting-room it suddenly opened and a woman came out."

He stopped – just for a moment – as if to let the people get the effect of his words. A rustle went over the room, but he looked as if he didn't notice it and went on as calm and natural as if he was telling us a fiction story.

"I probably wouldn't have noticed her if she hadn't given a suppressed cry and cowered back in the doorway. That made me look at her and, to my amazement, I saw it was Miss Hesketh's maid, Virginie Dupont."

Nobody expected it. If he'd wanted to spring a sensation he'd done it. We were all leaning forward with our mouths open.

"The moment I saw her I remembered that my wife had told me the woman had gone with Miss Hesketh. One glance into the waiting-room told me she was alone and I turned on her and told her I knew of the elopement and asked her what she was doing there. She was evidently terrified by my unexpected appearance, but seeing she was caught, she confessed that she knew all about it, in fact, that she had been instructed by Miss Hesketh to go to Philadelphia by the branch line, take a room in the Bellevue-Stratford, and wait there till her mistress appeared.

"I was enraged and let her see it, pushing her round to the car and ordering her into the back seat. I vaguely noticed that she carried a bag and wrap over her arm. She tried to excuse herself but I shut her up and took my seat at the wheel. There was no one on the platform as we went out.

"It took me over an hour to negotiate the distance between the Junction and the turnpike. The road was in a fearful condition. We ran into chuck holes and through water nearly to the hubs. Once the right front wheel dropping into a washout, the lamp struck a stump and was so shattered it had to be put out. My attention was concentrated on the path, especially after we left the open country and entered a thick wood, where, with one lamp out of commission, I had to almost feel my way.

"I said not a word to the woman nor she to me. It was not till I was once again in the open that I turned to speak to her and saw she was gone."

"Gone!" said one of the jury – a raw-boned, bearded old man like a farmer – so interested, he spoke right out.

"Yes, gone. I guessed in a moment what she had done. Either when I had stopped to put out the lamp or in one of the pauses while I was feeling my way through the wood she had slipped out and run. It would have been easy for her to hide in the dark of the trees. I glanced into the tonneau and saw that the things she had carried, the bag and the wrap, were also missing. She had been frightened and made her escape. Unfortunately, in the shock and horror of the next day the whole matter slipped my mind and she had time to complete her getaway, probably by the branch line early Sunday morning."

The Coroner here explained that inquiries had since been made at the branch line stations for the woman but nobody had been found who had seen her.

"I had no time to go back and look for her, and, anyway, it would have been useless, as she could have hidden from a sheriff's posse in the wood. Besides, my whole interest was focused on reaching the turnpike. I could see it before me, a long winding line between the dark edges of small trees. I turned into it and let the car out. Though the road has many turns I could have seen the lamps of a motor some distance ahead and I ran fast, looking neither to the right nor left but watching for approaching lights. On my ride back I met only a few vehicles, several farmers' wagons and the car of Dr Pease, the Longwood practitioner.

"I reached home about two and went at once to my wife's room. She was in a hysterical state and I stayed with her an hour or so trying to quiet her. When she was better I retired to my own apartment and at seven called up Walter Mills, a detective in New York, telling him to come to Longwood as soon as he could. By this time I was uneasy, not that I had any suspicion of a real tragedy, but the disappearance of Miss Hesketh alarmed me. I met Mills at the train and told him the situation and that I intended telephoning to Fiske at Bloomington, thinking they might have reached there by some other way. It was his suggestion that before any step was taken which might make the matter public, it would be well to communicate with Firehill and see if the servants knew anything. I did this and to my amazement learned that Reddy was there."

That is all of the Doctor's testimony that I need put down as the rest of it you know.

It left us in a sort of mixed-up surprise. No one could have told it better, no one could have been more sure about it or more quiet and natural. *But* – it seems like I ought to write that word in the biggest letters to give the idea of how it stood out in my mind.

Of all the stories it was the strangest and it was so *awfully* pat. I don't know how you feel about it, reading it as I've written it here, but I can say for myself, listening and watching that man tell it, I couldn't seem to believe it.

It was near to evening, the room getting dusk and the fire showing up large and bright when the jury brought in their verdict: "The deceased met her death at the hands of a person or persons unknown."

I walked back up Maple Lane. The night was setting in cold and frosty. The clouds had drawn off, the air was clear as crystal and full of the sounds of motor horns. Big and little cars passed me, jouncing over the ruts and swinging round the bend where the pine stood. I was looking up at it, black like a skeleton against the glow in the West, when a step came up behind me and a voice said:

"You're a good witness, Miss Morganthau."

It was that fresh kid Babbitts and I wasn't sorry to have him join me as I was feeling as if I'd been sitting in a tomb. He was serious too, not a wink about him now, his eyes on the ground, his hands dug down in the pockets of his overcoat.

"A strange case, isn't it?" he said.

"Awful strange," I answered.

"If it wasn't for your story of that man on the 'phone I think they'd arrest Dr Fowler tonight."

"Didn't you believe what he said?"

I wasn't going to give away my thoughts any more than I'd been willing to give away what I heard on the wire. And it seemed that he was the same, for he answered slow and thoughtful:

"I'm not saying what I believe or don't believe, or maybe it's better if I say I'm not ready yet to believe or disbelieve anything," – then he looked up at the sky, red behind the trees, and spoke easy and careless: "They say Miss Hesketh had a good many admirers."

"Do they?" was all he got out of me.

That made him laugh, jolly and boyish.

"Oh, you needn't keep your guard up now. Your stuff'll be in the papers tomorrow, and, take it from me, that fellow that sent the message is going to get a jar."

"The man I listened to?"

"Sure. He hasn't got the ghost of an idea anyone overheard him. Can't you imagine how he'll feel when he opens his paper and sees that a smart little hello girl was tapping the wire?"

It's funny, but I'd never thought of it that way. Why, he'd get a shock like dynamite! It got hold of me so that I didn't speak for a spell, thinking of that man reading his paper tomorrow – over his coffee or maybe going down in the L – and suddenly seeing printed out in black and white what he thought no one in the world knew except himself and that poor dead girl. Babbitts went on talking, me listening with one ear – which comes natural to an operator.

"We've been rounding up all the men that were after her – not that they were backward with their alibis – only too glad to be of service, thank you! Carisbrook was at Aiken, a lawyer named Dunham was up state trying a case; Robinson, a chap in a bank, was spending the week-end on Long Island. There was only one of them near here – man named Cokesbury. Do you know him?"

Both my ears got busy.

"Cokesbury," I said, sort of startled, "was Cokesbury at the Lodge last week?"

"He was and I know just what he did."

"What did he do?"

He laughed out as gay as you please, for he saw he'd got me just where he wanted.

"When I've tried to find out things from you you've turned me down."

"Aw, go on," I said coaxing, "don't you know by experience I'm no talking machine to give out every word that's said to me."

"I believe you," he answered, "and it'll be good for your character for me to set a generous example. Cokesbury was at the Lodge from last Saturday on the one-ten train to last Monday on the eight-twenty."

"Gee!" I said, soft to myself.

"You can quell those rising hopes," he replied. "He wasn't the man you heard."

"How do you know?"

"Because hearing that he was a friend of Miss Hesketh's, I spent part of yesterday at Azalea and found that Mr Cokesbury can prove as good an alibi as any of them."

"Did you see him?"

"No, he wasn't there and if he had been I wouldn't have bothered with him. I saw someone much better – Miner, the man who owns the Azalea Garage, where Cokesbury puts up his car. It appears that the trip before last Cokesbury broke his axle and had to have his car towed down to the garage and left there to be mended. When he came down Saturday he expected it to be done and when it wasn't, got in a rage and raised the devil of a row. He had to go out to his place in one of Miner's cars which left him there and went back for him Monday morning."

"Then he had no auto on Sunday."

"Miss Morganthau will take the head of the class," then he said, low, as if to someone beside him: "She's our prize pupil but we don't say it before her face for fear of making her proud," then back to me as solemn as a priest in the pulpit, "That is the situation reduced to its lowest terms – he had no car."

"Well that ends *him*," I said.

"So it seems to me. In fact Cokesbury gets the gate. I won't hide from you now that I went to Azalea because I'd heard a rumor of that talk on the phone and thought I'd do a little private sleuthing on my own. Didn't know but what I was destined to be the Baby Grand Burns."

"And nothing's come of it."

"Nothing, except that it drops Cokesbury out with a thud that's dull and sickening for me, but you can bet your best hat it's just the opposite for him."

"Well, I guess yes," I said and walked along wondering to myself whose voice that *could* have been.

VIII

After the inquest there was no more question about who was suspected. It was as if every finger in Longwood was raised and pointed to Mapleshade. The cautious people didn't say it plain – especially the shop-keepers who were afraid of losing custom – but those who had nothing to gain by keeping still came out with it flatfooted.

It wasn't only that nobody liked the Doctor, or believed his story, it was because the people were wild at what had been done. They wanted to find the murderer and put him behind bars and seeing that things pointed more clearly to Dr Fowler than to anybody else they pitched on him. All the gossip about the quarreling came out blacker than ever. The papers were full of it and the other worse stories, about Sylvia's allowance and the will of her father. There wasn't a bit of dirty linen in the Fowler household that wasn't washed and hung out on the line for the public to gape at, and some of it was dirtier when they'd got through washing than it had been before.

There were those who didn't scruple to say that the whole tragedy was a frame-up between Virginie Dupont and the Doctor. If you talked sensible to them and asked them how Virginie could have got word to him that Sylvia was running away, they'd just push that to one side, saying it could be explained some way, everything wasn't known yet – but one thing you *could* be sure of – the one person who knew the whereabouts of that French woman was Dr Daniel Fowler.

I believe there were some days after the inquest when, if there'd been an anarchist or agitator to stand on the postoffice steps and yell that Dr Fowler ought to be jailed, a crowd would have gathered, gone down to Mapleshade, and demanded him.

Fortunately there was no one of that kind around, and he stayed quiet in his home, not even coming to the village. Two days after the inquest I saw Anne and she said he and Mrs Fowler hadn't been out of the house – that they were in a state of siege what with reporters and the police and morbid cranks who hung round the grounds looking up at the windows.

That same evening I stayed overtime in the Exchange, lending a hand. The work was something awful, and Katie Reilly, the new girl, was most snowed under and on the way to lose her head. I wanted to see her through and I wanted the credit of the office kept up, but it's also true that I wanted to be on the job myself and hear all that was passing. Believe me, it was hard to quiet down in my bedroom at night after eight hours at the switchboard right in the thick of the excitement. Besides, I'd got to know the reporters pretty well and it was fun making them think I could give them leads and then guying them.

I liked Babbitts the best, but there were three others that weren't bad as men go. One was Jones, a tall thin chap like an actor, with long black hair hanging down to his collar, and Freddy Jasper, who was English and talked with an awful swell dialect, and a sallow-skinned, consumpted-looking guy called Yerrington who belonged on a paper as yellow as his face and always went round with a cigarette hanging from his lip like it was stuck on with glue.

It was nearly eight and work was slacking off when I started to go home. What with the jump I'd been on and listening to the gabbing round the door I'd forgotten my supper. It wasn't till I saw the Gilt Edge window with a nice pile of apples stacked up round a pumpkin, that I remembered I was hungry and walked over. There were only three people in the place, Florrie Stein, the waitress, and a woman with a kid in the corner.

I was just finishing my corn beef hash with a cup of coffee at my elbow and stewed prunes on the line of promotion when Soapy and Jones and Jasper came in and asked me if they could sit at my table. "Please yourself," said I, "and you'll please me," for politeness is one of the things I was bred up to, and they sat down, calling out their orders to Florrie Stein.

They naturally began talking about "the case" – it was all anybody talked about just then – and for all I knew so much about it, I generally picked up some new bits from them. So I went to the extravagance of three cents worth of jelly roll, not because I wanted it, but because I could crumb it up and eat it slow and not give away I was sitting on to listen.

"We can talk before you, Miss Morganthau," said Babbitts, "because while we all agree you're the belle of Longwood, we've found out by sad experience you're a belle without a tongue."

Florrie Stein, bringing the food then, they were silent till she'd set it out, and when she'd drawn off to the cashier's desk, they started in again. They were, so to speak, looking over Hines as a suspect.

"No, Hines won't fit," said Babbitts. "The presence of the jewelry on the body eliminates him. They've dug up his record and though the place he ran wasn't to be recommended for Sunday school picnics, the man himself seems to have been fairly decent."

"It's odd about the bag – the fitted bag and the jewelry gone from the room," said Jasper.

"The police have an idea that Virginie Dupont could tell something of them."

"Theft?"

"Theft on the side."

"Oh, pshaw!" said Jones, "what's the good of complicating things? If theft was committed it was a frame-up, part of a plot."

"You believe in this idea they've got in the village that Fowler and the French woman worked together?"

"I do – to my mind the murderer's marked as plain as Cain after he was branded on the brow or wherever it was."

Then Jasper spoke up. He's a nice quiet chap, not as fresh as the others. "Let's hear what you base that assertion on."

Jones forgot his supper and twisted round sideways in his chair, looking thoughtful up at the cornice:

"As I understand it, in a murder two things are necessary – a crime and a corpse; and in a murderer one, a motive. Now we have all three – the motive especially strong. If Miss Hesketh married, her stepfather lost his home and the money he had been living on, so he tried to stop her from marrying. Saturday night he heard that his efforts had failed. I fancy that on Sunday morning when he went for that auto drive he stopped at some village – not as yet located – and communicated with Virginie Dupont, who was in his pay. She, too, went out that morning, you may remember."

"There's a good deal of surmise about this," said Babbitts.

Jones gave him a scornful look.

"If the links in the chain were perfect Dr Fowler'd be eating his dinner tonight in Bloomington Jail."

"How do you account for Miss Hesketh – presupposing it was she – being on the train instead of the turnpike?" said Jasper.

"A change of plans," Jones answered calmly, "also not yet satisfactorily cleared up. To continue: Some time on Sunday the Doctor conceived the plan of ridding himself of all his cares – his troublesome stepdaughter, the disturbance of his home and his financial distress. *How*," he turned and looked solemnly at us, "fate played so well into his hands I can't yet explain – the main point is that it did. He met Miss Hesketh at the Junction, either by threats, persuasion or coercion made her enter his auto and carried her up the road to the turnpike."

"And now," said Babbitts, leaning his arms on the table, "we come to her appearance in the Wayside Arbor."

"We do," Jones replied, nodding his head. "You may remember that both Hines and his servant said there were twigs and leaves on the edge of her skirt and that her boots were muddy. Traces of this were still visible in her clothes when they found her body. She *did* get out of the automobile, but not so far from the turnpike as he said. Either he and she had some fierce quarrel and she ran from him in rage or terror, or he may have told the truth and she slipped out at the turn from the Riven Rock Road without his knowledge. Anyway she got away from him and ran for the only light she saw. There she telephoned Reddy, withholding the main facts from him, perhaps merely to save time, but cautioning him against letting anyone know of the message. That, as I see it, was a natural feminine desire to guard against gossip. When she thought Reddy was due she started out to meet him – and instead met the Doctor."

"Who'd been hanging about for a half-hour on the roadside?"

"Precisely. He killed her, concealed the body, and went home."

"Just a minute," said Yerrington – "what did he kill her with? The weapon used is a disputed point. Many think it was a farm implement. Did he go across lots to Cresset's and arm himself with a convenient spade or rake for the fatherly purpose of slaying his stepdaughter?"

But you couldn't phase Jones, he said as calm as a May morning:

"He *could* have done that. But I don't think he did. He didn't need it. The tool box of the car was nearer to hand. A large-sized auto wrench is a pretty formidable weapon, and a tire wrench – did you ever see one? One well-aimed blow of that would crush in anyone's head."

"Gentlemen, the evidence is all in," said Babbitts.

"Your case might hold water," said Jasper, "if it wasn't as full of holes as a sieve. Why, you can make out as good a one for almost anybody."

"Who, for example?" Jones asked.

"Well – take Reddy."

"Jack Reddy?" I said that, sitting up suddenly and staring at them with a piece of jelly roll halfway to my mouth.

"He's as good as another," said Jasper, and then he added sort of dreamy: "I believe I could work up quite a convincing case against Reddy, allowing for a hole here and there. But our illustrious friend here admits holes at this stage."

"Fire away," said Babbitts. "Give it to us, holes and all."

"Well – off the bat here it is. You may remember that no one saw him coming back from Maple Lane that night. There is no one, therefore, to deny that he may have had Miss Hesketh in the car with him. Instead of going back to Firehill, as he says he did, he followed his original plan of taking her by the turnpike."

"Right at the start I challenge that," said Babbitts. "She appeared at the Wayside Arbor at nine-thirty. The date in Maple Lane was for seven. Supposing she kept it and was on time – which is a stretch of the imagination – he would have had to travel one hundred and eighteen miles in two hours and a half."

"He could have done it."

"On a black, dark night? nearly forty-eight miles an hour?"

"You forget he knew the road and was driving a high-powered racing car. It's improbable but not impossible."

"I count that as a hole, but go on."

"Now in this hypothetical case we'll suppose that as that car flew over the miles the man and the woman in it had high words?"

"Hold on," said Jones, holding out his fork – "that's too big a hole. They were lovers eloping, not an old married couple."

"I'll explain that later. The high words inflamed and enraged the man to the point of murder and he conceived a horrible plan. As they neared the Wayside Arbor he told the woman something was wrong with the car and sent her to the place ostensibly to telephone, really to establish her presence there at a time when, had she been with him, she could hardly have got that far."

I jumped in there. I knew it was only fooling, but even so I didn't like hearing Mr Reddy talked about that way.

"Who did he send her to telephone to, Mr Jasper – himself?"

Babbitts laughed and jerked his head toward me.

"Listen to our little belle sounding the curfew on Jasper."

But Mr Jasper was ready.

"He could have done that, knowing his house was empty. Hines, you remember, said she wasn't five minutes in the booth. We've only Reddy's word for that message. We don't even know if she got a connection. I telephoned out to the Corona operator Saturday and she answered that there was no record of the message and she herself remembered nothing about it."

"But Sylvia," I said – "she told Hines she was expecting someone to come for her."

"Sylvia was eloping. Mightn't she have told Hines – who was curious and intrusive – what wasn't true?"

A sort of hush fell on us all. Babbitts's face and Jones's, from being just amused, were intent and interested.

"Go ahead, Jasper," said Babbitts, "if this isn't buying the baby a frock it's good yarning."

Jasper went on.

"Her story of the broken automobile *she* believed to be true. But she didn't want Hines to know who she was or what she was up to, so she invented the person coming to take her home. Why she sat so long there talking is – I'll admit – a hole, but I said in the beginning there would be some. The end is just like the end of Jones's case. She went back to Reddy and he killed her with, as our friend has suggested, one of the auto tools. Very soon after it would have been as that Bohemian – what's her name? – heard the scream at ten-ten."

"That's all very well," said Jones, "but before we go further I'd like you to furnish us with a motive."

"Nothing easier – jealousy."

"Jealousy!" I said, sudden and sharp.

"Jealousy in its most violent form. The lady in this case was a peculiar type – a natural born siren. She had made the man jealous, furiously jealous. *That* was the reason of the high words in the motor."

"Who was he jealous of?" It was I again who asked that.

Jasper turned round and looked at me with a smile.

"Why, Miss Morganthau," he said, "*you* gave us the clue to that. He was jealous of the man who made the date you heard on the phone. Don't you see," he said, turning to the others, "*that* man kept his date and Reddy came and found him there."

I can't tell what it was that fell on us and made us sit so still for a minute. All of us knew it was just a joke, but – for me, anyway – it was as if a cloud had settled on the room. Babbitts sat smoking a cigarette and staring at the rings he was making with his eyes screwed up. Presently, when Jones spoke, his voice had a sound like his pride was taken down.

"A great deal better than I expected, but it's simply riddled with holes."

Before Jasper could answer the door opened and Yerrington came in. The cigarette was hanging off his lip and as he said "Good evening" to me it wobbled but clung on. Then he pulled out a chair, sat down and, looking at the other three with a gleam in his eye, said:

"A little while ago Dr Fowler's chauffeur in dusting out his car found the gold mesh purse squeezed down between the back and the cushion."

IX

The finding of the gold purse established the fact that part, anyway, of the Doctor's story was true – the woman who had gone down to the junction and then disappeared *had* disappeared in his auto. Was she Sylvia Hesketh?

The general verdict was yes – Sylvia Hesketh, for some unknown reason, running away from her lover and her home. All the world knew now that she was wild and unstable, a girl that might take any whim into her head and act on the spur of the moment. There were theories to burn why she should have thrown down Reddy and slipped away alone, but those that knew her said she was a law unto herself and let it go at that.

The morning after that supper in the Gilt Edge, Anne came in to do the marketing and stopped at the Exchange. The room was empty but even so I had to whisper:

"Are they going to arrest the Doctor?"

"He's waiting," she whispered back.

"What do you make of it?"

"What I always have. I think the woman was Virginie. I think she took Sylvia's things and lit out on her own account."

"What does Mrs Fowler say?"

"She's going to offer a reward for the murderer. That's her way of answering. This last seems to have roused her. She knows now it's going to be a fight for her husband's liberty, perhaps his life. She's employing Mills and some other detectives and she keeps in close touch with them."

The next day the reward was made public. It was in all the papers and nailed up at the depot and in the post office, the words printed in black, staring letters:

TEN THOUSAND DOLLARS REWARD!

TO ANYONE DISCOVERING THE MURDERER OF THE LATE SYLVIA HESKETH, THIS SUM WILL BE PAID BY HER MOTHER, CONSTANCE GREY FOWLER, MAPLESHADE, NEW JERSEY.

Late that afternoon Babbitts came into the office. He was staying at the Longwood Inn, but it was the first time that day I'd seen him and after our supper together I'd begun to feel real chummy with him. Contrary to his usual custom he was short and preoccupied, giving me a number without more words and then banging shut the door of the booth. It got me a little riled and seeing he wasn't wasting any manners I didn't see why I should, so I lifted the cam and quietly listened in. Not that I expected to hear anything very private. The number he'd given was his paper.

The chap at the other end had a way of grunting, "I got you," no matter what was said. I'd heard *him* before and he had a most unnatural sort of patience about him, as if his spirit was broken forever taking messages off a wire.

"Say," says Babbitts, "I got a new lead – up country near Hines' place. I been there all morning. There's a farm up that way. Cresset's" – he spelled the name and the other one did his usual stunt – "Good people, years on the soil, self-respecting, stand high. Their house is about half a mile across woods and fields from the Wayside Arbor, lonely with a bad bit of road leading up from the pike. Do you hear?"

"Get on," said the voice.

"I stopped in there and had a séance with Mrs Cresset, nice woman, fat with a white apron. I said I was a tourist thirsting for a drink of milk."

The other one seemed to rouse up. "Did you thirst that bad?"

"For information – and I got it. She's been scared of the notoriety and has held back something which seems important. Her husband's been prying her up to the point of going to the District Attorney and she's agreed, but tried it on me first. Do you hear?"

"I got you."

"The night of the murder, about nine, a man knocked at her door saying he'd lost his way and wanting to know where he was, and how to get to the turnpike. She spoke to him from an upper window and couldn't see his face, the night being dark. All she could make out was that he was large and wore an overcoat. He told her his auto was in the road back of him and he'd got mixed up in the country lanes. The thing's funny, as there are very few roads that side of the pike."

"Hold on – what's that about pike?"

Babbitts repeated it and went on:

"Doesn't appear to have been in the least drunk – perfectly sober and spoke like a gentleman. She gave him the direction and here's what caught me – describes his voice as very deep, rich and pleasant, almost the same words the Longwood telephone girl used to describe the voice she overheard speaking to Miss Hesketh Saturday noon."

"Any more?"

"Impossible to identify man but says she'd know the voice again. He thanked her very politely – she couldn't lay enough stress on how good his manners were – and she heard him walk away, splashing through the mud."

There were a few ending-up sentences that gave me time to pull out a novel and settle down over it. I seemed so buried in it that when Babbitts put down his money I never raised my eyes, just swept the coin into the drawer and turned a page. He didn't move, leaning against the switchboard and not saying a word. With him standing there so close I got nervous and had to look up, and as soon as I did it he made a motion with his hand for me to lift my headpiece.

"If two heads are better than one," he said, "two ears must be; and the words I am about to utter should be fully heard to be appreciated."

Of course I thought he was going to tell me what he'd found out at Cresset's. It made me feel proud, being confided in by a newspaper man, and I pushed up my headpiece, all smiling and ready to be smart and helpful. He didn't smile back but looked and spoke as solemn as an undertaker.

"Miss Morganthau, yours is a very sedentary occupation."

Believe me I got a jolt.

"If you're asking me to violate the rules for that," I answered, "you're taking more upon yourself than I'll overlook from a child reporter with a head of hair like the Fair Circassian in Barnum & Bailey's."

"I speak only as one concerned for your health. A walk after business hours should be the invariable practice of those whose work forbids exercise."

"Thank you for your interest," says I, very haughty, "but it's well to look at home before we search abroad. The man who spends all his time riding in autos at the expense of the Press would be better employed exercising his own limbs than directing those of others. So start right along and walk quick."

He didn't budge, but says slow and thoughtful:

"Your remarks, Miss Morganthau, are always to the point. I'm going to take a walk this evening – say about seven-thirty."

"I hope you'll enjoy it," says I. "As for me, I'm going straight home to rest. I need it, what with my work and the ginks that stand round here taking up my time and running the risk of getting me fired" – the door handle clicked. I looked over my shoulder and saw a man coming in. "Which way?" I says in a whisper.

"Down Maple Lane," he whispers back, and I was in front of my board with my headpiece in place when the man came in.

We walked up and down Maple Lane for an hour, and it may amuse you to know that what that simple guy wanted was to tell me to listen to every voice on my wires.

I looked at him calm and pitiful. *Me*, that had been listening till, if your ears grow with exercise, mine ought to have been long enough to tie in a true lover's knot on top of my head!

There's a wonderful innocence about men in some ways. It makes you feel sorry for them, like they were helpless children.

Then he capped the climax by telling me about Mrs Cresset that morning – hadn't thought I'd heard a word. And as he told it, believing so honest that I didn't know, I began to feel kind of cheap as if I'd lied to someone who couldn't have thought I'd do such a thing. I didn't tell him the truth – I was too ashamed – but I made a vow no matter how sly I was to the others I'd be on the square with Babbitts. And I'll say right here that I've made good resolutions and broken them, but that one I've kept.

There's a little hill part way along the Lane where the road slopes down toward the entrance of Mapleshade. We stopped here and looked back at the house lying long and dark among its dark trees. The sky was bright with stars and by their light you could see the black patches of the woods and here and there a paler stretch where the land was bare and open. It was all shadowy and gloomy except where the windows shone out in bright orange squares. I pointed out to Babbitts where Sylvia's windows were, not a light in them; and then, at the end of the wing, four or five in a row that belonged to Mrs Fowler's suite. Her sitting-room was one of them where Anne had told me she and the Doctor always sat in the evenings.

"They're there now," I said. "What do you suppose they're doing?"

"Search me," said Babbitts, "I can't answer for another man, but if I was in the Doctor's shoes I'd be pacing up and down, with my Circassian Beauty hair turning white while you waited."

"Yes," I said, nodding. "I'll bet that's what he's doing. I can see them, surrounded by their riches, jumping every time there's a knock on the door, thinking that the summons has come."

And that shows you how you never can tell. For at that hour in that room the Doctor and Mrs Fowler were talking to Walter Mills, who had just come from Philadelphia, bringing them the first ray of hope they'd had since the tragedy. It was in the form of a diamond and ruby lavalliere that he had found the day before in a pawn shop and that Mrs Fowler had identified as Sylvia's.

Four days later a piece of news ran like wildfire through Longwood: Virginie Dupont had been arrested and brought to Bloomington.

They put her in jail there and it didn't take any third degree to get the truth out of her. She made a clean breast of it, for she was caught with the goods, all the lost jewelry being found in the place where she was hiding. It sent her to the penitentiary, and her lover, too, for whom – anyway she said so – she had robbed Sylvia's Hesketh's room on the night that Sylvia Hesketh disappeared.

If her story threw no light on the murder it exonerated the Doctor, for it fitted at every point with what he had said.

I'll write it down here, not in her words, but as I got it from the papers.

For some time she had been planning to rob Sylvia, but was waiting for a good opportunity. This came, when the Doctor, being out of the house, she discovered that an elopement was on foot. She had read Sylvia's letters, which were thrown carelessly about, and knew of the affair with Jack Reddy, and when on Sunday morning she was sent to the village to get a letter from Reddy she guessed what it was. Before giving it to Sylvia she went to her own room, opened the envelope with steam from a kettle, and read it. Then she knew that her chance had come.

When evening drew on she hung about the halls and saw Sylvia leave at a few minutes past six, carrying the fitted bag. The coast being clear, she went to her room, took an old black bag of her own and stole back. It was while she was getting this bag that the idea came to her of impersonating her mistress, as in that way she could steal some clothes. She secured the jewelry in a pocket hanging from her waist, took some false hair that Sylvia wore when the weather was damp, and covered her head with it, and selected a little automobile hat of which there were several, over all tying a figured black lace veil.

What she particularly wanted was a new Hudson seal coat that had been delivered a few days before. No one but herself and Miss Hesketh knew of this coat as there had been so much quarreling about Sylvia's extravagance, that the girl often bought clothes without telling. After putting it on she filled her bag with things from the bureau drawers, and just as she was leaving saw the gold mesh purse on the dresser and snatched it up.

All this was done like lightning and she thinks she left the house not more than twenty or twenty-five minutes after Sylvia. To catch the train she had to hurry and she ran up Maple Lane behind the hedge. She was nearing the village when she heard the whirr of an auto and through the hedge saw the two big headlights of a car, coming slowly down the Lane. For a moment she paused, peeking through the branches and made out that there was only one person in it, Jack Reddy.

She reached the station only a few minutes before the train came in. As she had a ticket, she stood at the dark end of the platform, not moving into the light till the engine was drawing near. Then Jim Donahue saw her and came up, addressing her as Miss Hesketh. She had often tried to imitate Sylvia's voice and accent which she thought very elegant, and she did so now, speaking carefully and seeing that Jim had no doubt of her identity. On the ride to the Junction she had only murmured "Good evening" to Sands, being afraid to say more.

At the Junction she was going to get off, take the branch line to Hazelmere and transfer there to the Philadelphia Express. In the women's waiting-room, which would probably be deserted at that hour, she intended taking off Sylvia's coat and hair and reappearing as the modest and insignificant lady's maid. She had thought this out in the afternoon, deciding that Sylvia would probably communicate with her mother in the morning and that the theft would then be discovered. Inquiries started for the woman who had been seen on the train would lead to nothing, as that woman would have dropped out of sight at the Junction.

Everything worked without a hitch. The waiting-room was empty and she had ample time to take off the hair and put it in the bag, hang the coat over her arm with the lining turned out, and even pinch the small, soft hat into another shape. No one would have thought the woman who went into the waiting-room was the woman who came out.

And then came the first mishap – as she opened the door she stepped almost into Dr Fowler. She was terror stricken, but even then neither her luck nor her wits left her, for almost the first sentence he uttered showed her that he knew of the elopement and gave her a lead what to say. She must have been a pretty nervy woman the way she jumped at that lead. Right off the bat she invented the story about being sent by Sylvia to Philadelphia – to wait there at the Bellevue-Stratford.

The Doctor was furious and ordered her into his auto. There was nothing for it but to obey and in she got, sitting in the back. As she was stepping up, he close beside her, she remembered the gold mesh purse plain in her hand. Like a flash she bent forward and jammed it down between the back and seat.

The ride up the Riven Rock Road was just as the Doctor described it. It was after the lamp had been broken and he was back in the car starting it up, that she slipped out. She was determined to get away with all her loot and took the bag and coat with her, but between the hurry and fear of the moment forgot the purse.

She wandered through the woods till she saw a small scattering of lights which she took for one of the branch line stations. When the dawn came she had lost some of her nerve and felt it was too risky to carry the extra things. So she hid them at the root of a tree, took off the hat, tying the veil over her head, and walked across the fields to the station. As it was Monday morning there were a lot of laborers, men and women, on the platform. She mingled with them, looking like them in her muddy clothes and tied up head, and got away to Hazelmere without being noticed.

She was feeling safe in her furnished room in Philadelphia when she read of the murder in the papers. That scared her almost to death and she lay as close as a rabbit in a burrow, afraid to go out and cooking her food on a gas ring. It was the man she had stolen for who gave her away. When she refused to raise money on the jewels, he stole the lavalliere and pawned it.

Under the trees where she said she'd left them, the police found the coat and hat. Beside them was the bag stuffed full of lingerie, gloves and silk stockings, and with the false hair crowded down into the inside pocket.

Besides clearing the Doctor her confession threw light on two important points – one that Sylvia had left the house at a little after six, and the other that Reddy had been at the meeting place at the time he said.

X

After the excitement of the French woman's arrest there was a sort of lull. For a few days people thought we were going to move right on and lay our hands on the murderer. But outside of proving that the Doctor wasn't the guilty one the crime was no nearer a solution than it had been the day it happened. Though there was still a good deal of talk about it, it began to die down in the public interest and it was then that the papers got to calling it "The Hesketh Mystery" in place of "The Hesketh Murder."

The reporters left the Inn and went back to live in town, coming in every few days to snoop around for any new items that might have turned up. Babbitts came oftener than the others and stayed later, and he and I had several more walks. We were getting to be like partners in some kind of secret business, meeting after dark, and pacing along the roads round the village, with the stars shining overhead and the ground hard and crumbly under our feet.

If you'd met us you'd have set us down for a pair of lovers, walking side by side under the dark of the trees. But if you'd followed along and listened you'd have got cured of that romantic notion mighty quick. Our flirtation was all about evidence, and leads, and clues – not so much as a compliment or a baby stare from start to finish. I don't believe if you'd asked Babbitts he could have told you whether my eyes were brown or blue, and as for me – outside his being a nice kid he didn't figure out any more important than the weathervane on the Methodist Church.

It was "the case" that drew us together like a magnet drawing nails. We'd speculate about it, look at it all round as if it was something we had hold of in our hands. I guess it was the mysteriousness of it that attracted him, and the reward, too. There was more in it for me as you know – but he never got a hint of *that*.

It was one evening, nearly four weeks after the murder that he gave me a shock – not meaning to, of course, for even then I'd found out he was the kind that wouldn't hurt a fly. We were talking of Jack Reddy, who we'd seen that evening in the village, the first time since the inquest.

"You know," said Babbitts, "it's queer but I keep thinking of that yarn of Jasper's, that evening in the Gilt Edge."

I drew away like he'd stuck a pin into me.

"Why do you think about *that*?" I asked loud and sharp.

"Why," he said, slow as if he was considering, "I suppose because it was so plausible. And I've been wondering if many other people have thought of it."

"I guess they have," I answered kind of fierce; "there's fools enough in the world, God knows, to think of anything. I make no doubt there's people who've tried to work out that *I* did it, the reward tempting them to lies and sin."

Babbitts looked at me surprised.

"What's there to get mad about?" he asked. "I'm not for a moment suggesting that Reddy really had any hand in it. Why, he could no more have killed that girl than *I* could kill *you*."

I simmered down – it was awful sweet the way he said it.

"Then you oughtn't to be casting suspicions on an innocent man," I said, still grouchy.

"Oh, you're such a little pepper pot. Do you think for a moment I'd say this to anybody but you. Look at me!" I looked into his eyes, clear as a baby's in the starlight. "If you believe

I'm the sort of fellow who'd put a slur on Reddy I wonder you'll come out this way and walk with me."

I smiled, I couldn't help it, and Babbitts, seeing I was all right again, tucked his hand inside my arm and we walked on, very friendly. Being ignorant of the true state of my feelings, he went straight back to the subject.

"Now understand that I mean nothing against Reddy and that I've never said this to a soul but you, but ever since the inquest there's been one thing that's puzzled me – the length of time he was out that night."

"He explained that," I said.

"I know he did, and everybody's accepted his explanation. But seven hours in a high-powered racing car! He could have gone to Philadelphia, taken in a show and come back."

"But he told all about it," I insisted.

"He did," said Babbitts, "but I'll tell you something, Miss Morganthau – between ourselves not to go an inch farther – Reddy's story impressed me as the undiluted truth till he got to *that* part of it."

"What do you mean?" I said, low, and being afraid I was going to tremble I pulled my arm away from him.

"This – I was watching him very close, and when he began to talk about that night ride, some sort of change came over him. It was very subtle, I never heard anyone speak of it, but it seemed to me as if he was making an effort to give an impression of frankness. The rest of his testimony had the hesitating, natural tone of a man who is nervous and maybe uncertain of his facts, but when he came to that he – well, he looked to me as if he was internally bracing himself, as if he was on dangerous ground and knew it."

If I'd been able to speak as well as that those were exactly the words I would have used. I cleared my throat before I answered.

"Looks like to me, Mr Babbitts, that you ought to be writing novels instead of press stories."

"Oh, no," he said careless, "but, you see, I've been on a number of cases like this and a fellow gets observant. It's queer – the whole thing. If that French woman's evidence is to be trusted Miss Hesketh *did* leave the house early to keep that date with the Voice Man."

I didn't say a word, looking straight before me at the lights of Longwood through the trees. Babbitts, with his hands in his pockets swinging along beside me, went on:

"That's what's made me think of Jasper's hypothetical case. Do you remember? He said Reddy'd come down to the meeting place, found Miss Hesketh with the other man and got into a Berserker rage. Say what you like, it does work out."

When he bid me goodnight at Mrs Galway's side door he wanted to know why I was so silent? Even if I'd wanted to give a reason I hadn't one to give. Don't you believe for a minute I was really worried – it was just that I hated anyone even to yarn that way about Jack Reddy. Poor me – if I'd known then what was coming!

It began to come two days later, the first shadow that was going to darken and spread till – but I'm going on too quick.

I'd just had my lunch, put away my box and swept off the crumbs, when I got a call for the depot from the Rifle Run Camp. That's a summer resort, way up in the hills beyond Hochalaga Lake. The voice, with a brogue on it as rich as butter, was Pat Donahue's, Jim's eldest son, a sort of idle scamp, who'd gone up to the camp to work last summer and had stayed on because there was nothing to do – at least that's what Jim said.

I made the connection and listened in, not because I was expecting anything worth hearing, but because I wasn't taking any chances. I guess Pat Donahue was the last person anyone would expect to come jumping into the middle of the Hesketh mystery – but that's what he did, with both feet, hard.

I didn't pay much attention at first and then a sentence caught my ear and I grew still as a statue, my eyes staring straight in front, even breathing carefully as if they could hear.

It was Pat's voice, the voice answering Jim's at the Depot:

"Me and Bridger was in to Hochalaga Lake yesterday forenoon, fishin' through the ice. Can you hear me, Paw?"

"Fine. Are you payin' for a call to tell me you're that idle you have to play at fishin'?"

"Jest you listen close and hear me before you come back. I seen in the papers that Miss Hesketh that was murdered had one glove lost. Do you mind what the one that wasn't lost looked like?"

"Sure I do – why shouldn't I? Didn't I see it at the inquest?"

"Will you be answering me instead of tellin' me what you saw?"

"Ain't I doin' it? It was a left-hand glove, light gray with three pearl buttons and a furrener's name stamped in the inside."

"Well, then, I got the feller to it – right hand. I found it on the wharf at the lake, in front of the bungalow. Seeing that there's ten thousand dollars reward offered, I thought I'd be a blowin' in the price of a call to tell you, though it's so ungrateful ye are for the news I'm sorry I done it. But I'll not bother you no more, for it's in to the District Attorney I'll be goin' with the evidence."

That was what he did, that very afternoon. By the next day everybody in Longwood knew how Pat Donahue had found Sylvia Hesketh's missing glove on the wharf just in front of the Reddy bungalow. There was a person who didn't close an eye that night, and I guess you know what her name was.

Gee, those were awful days that followed! When I think of them now I can feel a sort of sinking come back on me and my face gets stiff like it was made of leather and couldn't limber up for a smile. Each morning I'd get up scared sick of what I was going to hear that day, and each evening I'd go to bed filled with a darkness as black as the night outside.

I couldn't believe it and yet – well, I'll tell you and you can judge for yourself.

The police went out to Hochalaga and made a thorough examination of the house and its surroundings.

The bungalow stood at one end of the lake right on the shore, with a little wharf jutting out in front of it into the water. The door opened into a big living-room, furnished very pretty and comfortable with green madras curtains at the windows, a green art rug on the floor, and wicker chairs with green denim cushions. At one side was a big brick fireplace with a copper kettle hanging on a crane and over in a corner was a desk with a telephone on it. Along the walls were bookcases full of books and in the center was a table with chairs drawn up at either side of it.

The police noticed right off that it didn't have the damp, musty feel of a place shut up through a long spell of rain. The air was cold and dry and they could scent the odor of wood fires and a slight faint smell of cigar smoke. Then they saw that the fireplace was piled high with ashes and that several cigarette ends were scattered on the hearth. On the center table was a shaded lamp and near it a match box with burnt matches strewn round on the floor. The desk drawer was open and the papers inside all tossed and littered about as if someone had gone through them in a hurry. Two armchairs stood on either side of the table and another was in front of the fireplace. All over the floor were earth stains as if muddy feet had been walking about. There were no signs that the place had been broken into – windows and doors were locked and the locks in good condition.

Outside against the wall of the house they found a pile of broken china, what seemed to be the remains of a tea set. It was not till the search was nearly ended that one of the men, studying the grass along the roadside for traces of footprints, came on a gasoline drum hidden among the bushes.

But that wasn't the worst – leading up the road to within a few yards of the wharf were the tracks of auto wheels. At the time when these tracks were made the road was deep in mud which, about the wharf, had evidently been a regular pool. The driver of the motor had stopped his car at the edge of this, got out and walked through it to the bungalow. Clear as if they had been cast in plaster his footprints went from where the ruts ended to the edge of the wharf. There, just at the corner of the planks, three small, pointed footprints met them – a woman's. Either the man had carried the woman or she had picked her way along the grass by the roadside, and joining him on the planks had made a step or two into the soft earth. On the wharf the prints were lost in a broken caking of mud. The man's went back to the car, close to where they had come from it, and they returned as they had come – alone.

Jack Reddy's shoes fitted the large prints and Sylvia Hesketh's the small ones!

It came on Longwood with an awful shock. The faces of the people were all dull and dazed looking, as if they were knocked half silly by a blow. They couldn't believe it – and yet there it was! The papers printed terrible headlines – "The Earth gives up a Murderer's Secret" – and "Jack Frost versus Jack Reddy." There were imaginary accounts of how Mr Reddy could have done it, and Jasper, in his paper, had a long article worked out like the story he'd told us that night in the Gilt Edge, but with all the holes filled up. Everything was against Mr Reddy, even the telephone message that Sylvia had sent him from the Wayside Arbor couldn't be traced. The Corona operator could remember nothing about it and there was no record – only Jack Reddy's word and nobody believed it.

They had him up before the District Attorney and his examination was published in the papers. I can't put it all down – it's not necessary – but it was bad. After I read it I sat still in my room, feeling seasick and my face in the glass frightened me.

When they asked him if he had been at the bungalow that night he said he had, he had gone there after he had given up his hunt for Sylvia.

"Why didn't you say this at the inquest?" was asked.

He answered "that he hadn't thought it was necessary – that—" then he stopped as if he wasn't sure and after a moment or two said: "I didn't see that it threw any light on the murder, as I was alone."

"You wished to conceal the fact that you were there, then?"

To that he answered sharp:

"I did not – but I saw no reason to give my movements in detail, as they were of no importance."

"Why did you go there?"

"I was angry and excited and it was a place where I could be quiet."

Asked how long he had been in the bungalow he said he wasn't sure – it might have been an hour or two. He had lit the fire and sat in front of it thinking and smoking cigarettes.

"Didn't you hunt in the desk for something?"

He answered with a sort of shrug as if he'd forgotten.

"Oh, yes – I was hunting for a bill I thought I left there."

To the questions about Sylvia – whether she had been there with him – he answered almost violently that she had not, that he had not seen her there or anywhere else that night.

"Did you notice any footprints in the mud when you came?"

"I did not."

"There were no evidences on the wharf or in the house of anyone having been there before you?"

"None. The bungalow was locked and undisturbed."

Then they switched off on to the gasoline drum and asked him if he had filled the tank there and he said he might have but he didn't remember.

"Was it dark when you left the place?"

"No – very bright moonlight."

"You remember that?"

"Yes. I recollect thinking the ride back would be easier than the ride up in the dark."

"Why did you say at the inquest that you filled the tank somewhere on the turnpike?"

"I suppose I thought I had. In the angry and excited state I was in small things made no impression on me. I had no clear memory of where I'd done it."

All the papers agreed that his testimony was unsatisfactory and made much of his manner, which, under an effort to be calm, showed a spasmodic, nervous violence.

A day later he was arrested at Firehill and taken to Bloomington jail to await indictment by the Grand Jury.

That night – shall I ever forget it! I heard the sounds in the street dying away and then the silence, the deep, lovely silence that comes over the village at midnight. And in it I could hear my heart beating, and as I lay with my eyes wide open, I could see on the darkness like a picture drawn in fire, Jack Reddy in the electric chair.

XI

Looking back now I can remember dressing the next morning, all trembly and with my hands damp, and my face in the glass, white and pinched like an East Side baby's in a hot wave. But there wasn't anything trembly about the thinking part of me. That was working better than it had ever worked before. It seemed to be made of steel springs going swift and sure like an engine that went independent of the rest of my machinery.

And, thank God, it did work that way, for it had thought of something!

The idea came on me in the second part of the night, flashed out of the dark like a wireless. I'd been wondering about the man who made the telephone date with Sylvia – the Unknown Voice they'd got to calling him. People thought as Jasper had said, that Reddy had found her with this man and there had been a terrible scene. But whatever had happened the Unknown Voice was the clew to the mystery. The police had tried to locate him, tried and failed. Now *I* was going to hunt for him.

My plan was perfectly simple. From what I had seen myself and heard from Anne Hennessey I was sure I knew every lover that Sylvia had had. I was going to call each one of them up on the phone and listen to their voices, and I wasn't going to tell a soul about it. Everybody would say – just as you say as you read this – "but all those men gave satisfactory alibis." I knew that as well as anyone, but it didn't cut any ice with me, I didn't care what they'd proved. I was going to hear their voices and see for myself. If I was successful, then I'd tell Babbitts and have him advise me what to do. I'd heard Jack Reddy had retained Mr Wilbur Whitney, the great criminal lawyer, but I wouldn't have known whether to go to him or the police or the District Attorney and if I did it at all I wanted to do it right.

Now that there were three of us in the Exchange my holiday had been changed to Monday, and I made up my mind not to put my plan into execution till that day. I didn't want to be hurried, or confused, by possible interruptions, and also I wanted to hear the voices at short range and could do that better from the city. I telephoned over to Babbitts that I'd be in town Monday to do some shopping, and he made a date to meet me at the entrance of the Knickerbocker Hotel and dine with me at some joint near Times Square.

Monday morning I was up bright and early and dressed myself in my best clothes. From the telephone book I got the numbers of the four men who were known to have been Sylvia's lovers and admirers – Carisbrook, Robinson, Dunham and Cokesbury. I had found out from Anne what their businesses were and I had no trouble in locating them. With the slip of paper in my purse I took the ten-twenty train and was in town before midday.

On the way over I worked out what I'd say to each of them. I was going to ask Carisbrook, who was a soft, dressed-up guy, if he knew where Mazie Lorraine, a manicure who'd once been in the Waldorf, had moved to. It was nervy but I wanted to give him a dig, he having put on airs and treated me like a doormat. Robinson was easy – he had a common name and I'd got the wrong man. Excuse *me*, please, awful sorry. Dunham was a lawyer and I was a dressmaker that a customer wouldn't pay. And Cokesbury was easy, too – I'd heard Cokesbury Lodge was for rent and was looking for a country place.

I got Carisbrook first and he was as mad as a hornet.

"I don't know what you're talking about. *Manicure*? I don't know any manicure called Lorraine or anything else. I've never been manicured in the Waldorf – or any other hotel – in the city. The woman is a liar—" and so forth and so on, sputtering and fizzing along the wire. I had hard work not to laugh and in the middle of it I hung up, for he had a thin, high squeak on him like an old maid scared by a mouse.

Robinson was a sport, I liked *him* fine:

"Don't apologize. It's the penalty of being called Robinson. Still there's a bright side to every cloud. It might have been Smith, you know."

It wasn't Robinson. He talked with a dialect that sounded like Jasper's, English, I guess.

Dunham was very smooth and awful hard to get rid of. He kept on asking questions and I had to think quick and speak unnaturally intelligent. In the middle of it – I'd got what I wanted – I said it was too complicated to tell over the phone and I'd be in tomorrow at two and my name was Mrs Pendleton.

It wasn't Dunham.

When I tackled Cokesbury I ran into the first snag. I tried his office and a real pleasant young man (you get to know a young voice from an old one) asked me what I wanted. I said business, and he answered:

"What is the nature of your business, Madam?"

"I'd rather tell that to Mr Cokesbury," I said.

"Mr Cokesbury doesn't like to be interrupted in the office. If you'll tell me what you want to see him about—"

"Say, young feller," said I, in a cool, classy way, "suppose we stop this pleasant little talk, and you trot into Mr Cokesbury and say a lady's waiting on the wire."

"Very well," he answered, calm and cheerful, "I'll do just as you say."

There was a wait and then he was back.

"Mr Cokesbury says it's impossible for him to come to the phone and will you kindly tell me what your business is."

"I guess I'll have to wait till he's not so busy," I answered, languid, like I've heard ladies when they're mad and don't want to show it, and I hung up.

Afterward I saw I'd made a mistake, for, when I called up two hours later that polite guy was still on the job and handed me the same line of talk.

I went into a drugstore and looked up Cokesbury – Edward L., residence. It was in the East Fifties and at six I tried him there.

I drew a man that I guess was a servant:

"Is Mr Cokesbury home?"

"Who is it?"

"That doesn't matter. I want to know if he's home."

"I don't know, ma'am. Will you please give me your name?"

"Say, you're not taking the census or compiling a new directory, you're answering the phone. Tell Mr Cokesbury a party wants to see him on business."

"I have orders, ma'am, not to bother Mr Cokesbury with messages unless I know who they're from," said the voice, and then I knew he *was* there.

"I'm sure he'll come if you say it's a *lady*," I said, sort of coaxing and sweet.

"I'll try, ma'am," said the voice, and I could hear the echo of his feet as he walked off.

Presently he was back.

"Beg pardon, ma'am, but Mr Cokesbury says he can't possibly come and please to give me the message."

By that time I was getting mad.

"You ought to get double pay, for you seem to be a District Messenger boy as well as a butler. If it's not too much trouble would you mind telling me what Mr Cokesbury's friends do when they want a word with him over the phone?"

"They tell the butler who they are and what they want, ma'am. That's the orders in this house. Goodbye."

When Babbitts and I were sitting at a table in a little dago joint near Broadway, I couldn't help but tell him what I'd been doing.

He looked at me with his eyes as big as half-dollars and then began to laugh.

"Well, what do you make of that? Spending your holiday and your nickels rounding up a lot of men that rounded themselves up weeks ago."

"I want to get that voice."

"But everyone of them have proved that voice couldn't be theirs."

"Maybe they did," said I, "but I want to know it myself."

"Listen to her," he said, looking round the table as if a crowd was collected, "calmly brushing aside the police, the detectives, the might of the law and the strong arm of the press."

"And anything else that stands round trying to discourage me."

"Far be it from me to discourage you in any eccentricity that may develop. But there's no need in following up Cokesbury, for we know that he was marooned in Cokesbury Lodge."

"I don't care what we know. The only things I believe are the things I see myself."

"Thomas!" he said, laughing, and I didn't see any sense in his calling me that, but he often said things I wasn't on to. "Do you intend to camp on his trail all night?"

"I do," I answered. "As soon as you get through lapping up that red ink I'm going to go to the nearest pay station and ring up Edward L., residence."

"I'll toddle along," he said. "Anything goes with me that adds to the entertainment of Mary McKenna Morganthau."

He held up his glass as if he was drinking a toast, and something about the look of him – I don't know what – made me get all embarrassed. It never happened before and it took me so by surprise I blushed and was glad I'd dropped my gloves on the floor so I could bend down and hide how red my face was.

I tried Edward L., residence, at a drug store on Broadway and again I drew that butler gink, who was sort of sassy and hung up quick. Then we walked along and I could see that Babbitts was getting interested.

"Tell you what," he said, "that servant knows you. I'll make the connection, say I want to see Cokesbury on business, and if I get him, hand on the receiver to you."

We fixed it that way, went into a hotel, and I stood at the door of the booth while Babbitts got the house. Standing at his elbow I could see he was up against the same proposition as I had been. He finally had to say he wanted to see Mr Cokesbury about renting Cokesbury Lodge.

He turned to me with his hand over the mouthpiece and said:

"He's there and he won't come."

"Has the servant gone to get him?"

"Yes. He wouldn't say whether his boss was home or not, but his willingness to take the message gave him away. Now stand close and if it's a new voice I won't say a word, just get up and let you slide into my place." He started and turned back to the instrument. "Yes. What?" I could see a look of surprise come over his face. "Soon? You don't know – in a few days. Hasn't any idea of renting. Thanks. That's all – goodbye."

He hung up and turned to me:

"It was the servant. Cokesbury hasn't any intention of renting and is leaving for Europe."

"For Europe!" I cried out. "*When?*"

"The man didn't know exactly. He said he thought in a few days."

We walked down the street silent and thoughtful. The only feeling I had at first was disappointment. I didn't get the whole thing clear as Babbitts did. It came on him all in a minute, he told me afterward.

We were on Broadway as light as day with the signs and people walking by us and crowding in between us as if they were hurrying to catch trains. I felt Babbitts' hand go round my arm, steering me into a side street. It was darker there and there were only a few passers-by. We slackened up and still with his hand around my arm, he bent his face down toward my ear and said low, as if he was afraid someone was listening:

"Kiddo, are you on?"

"To what?"

"Cokesbury. Don't you get it? He won't answer the phone."

"Do you mean he won't answer at all?"

"Not unless it's someone he knows. He's got his clerks in the office holding the fort and his servants at home."

We were just under a lamp and I stopped with my mouth falling open, for sudden, like a flash of light, it came to me.

"Soapy!" I gasped and wheeled round on him. His face bent down toward me, was intent like a hunting dog's when it sees a bird, his eyes, bright and fixed, looking straight into mine.

"You've made the first real discovery in this case, Molly Morganthau. Cokesbury's scared, d—d scared, so scared he's lost his nerve and is lighting out to Europe."

We walked round into Bryant Park and sat down on a bench. We were so excited we didn't notice anything – that I'd grabbed Babbitt's hand and kept hold of it, that it was freezing cold, that we'd got on a bench with a drunk all huddled up on the other end. We were as certain as if he'd confessed it that Cokesbury was the Unknown Voice and that he'd killed Sylvia Hesketh. We just brushed his alibi aside as if he'd never made one and planned how I was to hear him before he got away to Europe. We laid plots there in the dark, sitting close together to keep warm, with the drunk all lopped over and muttering to himself on the seat beside us.

When Babbitts left me at the Ferry we'd fixed it that he was to call me up the next day and tell me what he'd done in town and I was to tell him what I'd accomplished at my end of the line.

The next morning I tried Cokesbury's office with the same results. At one Babbitts called me and said he'd tried twice to get him as a test and been told that Mr Cokesbury wasn't down today and his whereabouts were unknown. By inquiries at the steamship offices he'd found that Our Suspect – that's what we called him on the wire – had taken passage on the *Caronia* for the following Saturday. That was four days off – four days to hear the man who wouldn't answer the phone.

That afternoon I had an idea, called up Anne Hennessey and asked her to meet me at the Gilt Edge for supper. She came and afterward in my room at Galway's I told her – I had to, but she's true-blue and I knew it – and she agreed to help. She was to come to the Exchange the next morning, call up Cokesbury and say she was Mrs Fowler, who wanted to bid him goodbye before he left. While she spoke – imitating Mrs Fowler – I was to listen. We did it – though she'd have lost her job if she'd been found out – and I heard the clerk tell her that Mr Cokesbury wasn't in his office, that he didn't know where she could find him, and that it was very little use trying to get him on the phone as he was so much occupied prior to his departure.

When Anne came out of the booth I was crying. I guess I never before in my life had my nerves as strung up as they were then.

It wasn't long after that that I had a call from Babbitts. He'd been able to do nothing. When he heard of my last attempt he said:

"He's not answering any calls at all now. His own mother couldn't get him. It's no use trying that line any more. We've got to think up some other way."

That was Wednesday – I had only three days. Three days and I hadn't an idea how to do it. Three days and Jack Reddy was waiting indictment in Bloomington jail. We couldn't stop Cokesbury going or get anybody else to stop him unless we could light on something more definite than a hello girl's suspicions.

XII

Thursday afternoon I was sitting in the Exchange, feeling as if the bottom had fallen out of the world. I hadn't given up yet – I'm not the giving-up kind – but I *couldn't* think of anything else to do. I'd tossed on my bed all night thinking, I'd dressed thinking, I'd tried to eat thinking, I'd put in the plugs and made the connections thinking – and nothing would come.

Two days more – two days more – two days more – those three words kept going through my head as if they were strung on an endless chain.

And then – isn't it always that way in life? Just when you're ready to throw up the sponge and say you're beaten, Bang – it comes!

It came in the shape of a New York call for Azalea.

Like a dream, for I was pretty nearly all in, I could hear the operator's voice:

"That you, Longwood? Give me Azalea, 383."

And then me answering:

"All right. Azalea 383. Wait a minute."

I plugged in and heard that queer grating sound as if the wires were rubbing against each other:

"Hello, New York. All right for Azalea 383."

And then a woman's voice, clear and small.

"Here's your party. Just a minute. There you are – Azalea 383."

Then a man's voice far away as if it might be in Mars:

"Hello, is that Azalea 383?"

"Yep – the Azalea Garage," that was close and plain.

"This is Mr Cokesbury's butler—" Believe *me*, I came to life. "Cokesbury, Cokesbury of Cokesbury Lodge – get it?"

"Yep."

"I've a message for Miner – the manager."

"Fire away, I'm Miner."

"He wants to know if you found a raincoat in that auto he had from you last time he was down? *Raincoat*, waterproof. Do you hear?"

"Yes sir, I hear perfect. We've got it and I'd 'a' sent it back but I thought he'd be down again any time and it was just as well to keep it here."

"That's all right. The coat doesn't matter – but he's lost a key that does. Thinks maybe he left it in the pocket. Have you found any key?"

"I haven't looked. Hold the wire while I see?"

There was a pause while I prayed no one would come in or call up. My prayer was answered. There was nothing to interrupt when I heard the garage man's voice again:

"The key's there."

"Good work! Mr Cokesbury's had the house here upside down looking for it. He wants you to do it up careful and give it to Sands the Pullman conductor on the six-twenty tonight. I'll come across and get it off him at Jersey City."

"All right. Will I send the raincoat along, too?"

"No, he don't want that. He's goin' to Europe Saturday and I guess he's calculating to buy a new one. Thanks for your trouble. Goodbye."

"Goodbye."

I dropped the cam, sat tight, and thought. People kept coming in and out and calls came flashing along the wires and I worked swift and steady like an operator that's got no thought but for what's before her.

But my mind was working like a steam engine underneath. How could I get him – how could I get him? It was as if I had two brains, one on the top that went mechanical like a watch and one below that was doing the real business.

Before the afternoon was over I'd decided on a line of action.

I called up Katie Reilly and asked her if she'd relieve me at five-thirty instead of six – that I'd an invitation to go down to a party at Jersey City and I was keen to get there early. She agreed and at six I was on the platform of the station waiting for the New York train.

I took a seat in the common coach and at Azalea watched from the window and saw a man on the platform give Sands a packet. I knew Sands well and when he passed back through my car nodded to him and he stopped and stood in the aisle talking.

It wasn't long before I said, careless:

"I hear Cokesbury Lodge is for rent."

"I ain't heard it," said Sands, "but I ain't surprised. Now he's sent his family away he don't want a house that size on his hands."

"Has he been down lately?"

"No – not for – lemme see – it's several weeks. Yes – the last time was the Sunday before Sylvia Hesketh's murder."

I knew all that but it doesn't do to jump at what you're after too quick.

"Lucky for him he could prove his car was on the blink that time," I said, looking languid out of the window.

"Sure. He and Reddy were the only ones of her fellers within striking distance. But no one ever'd suspicion Cokesbury. He ain't the murderin' kind, too jolly and easy. I hear he's goin' to Europe."

"Is he now? Where'd you hear that?"

"From Miner, that runs the Azalea Garage. He come down to the station just now and gave me a package. Something

Cokesbury left in the motor the last time he was down. I'm to hand it over to his servant at Jersey City."

"Is it love letters that he don't want to leave behind?"

"No, I guess he's careful of them. Here it is," he drew out of his breast pocket an envelope with Cokesbury's name and address written on it and held it out to me. "That ain't no love letter."

I pinched it.

"It's a key. It may open the desk where the love letters are kept."

"I guess he's too fly to keep any dangerous papers like that around."

"Yes," I says, "they might set the house on fire."

"Well, ain't you the sassy kid," says he and then the train slowing up for a station he walked on up the aisle.

In the Jersey City depot I went like a streak for the Telephone Exchange. My one chance was to catch him at dinner and I gave the operator the number of his house. When she pointed to the booth I was trembling like a leaf.

The voice that answered me was a woman's – Irish – the cook's, I guess. She began right off: "Yes, this is Mr Cokesbury's residence, but you can't see him."

"Wait," I almost screamed, scared that she was going to disconnect, "this is important. It's about a key I've just found. If Mr Cokesbury's there tell him a lady wants to see him about a key she picked up a few minutes ago on the New Jersey train."

"All right. Hold the wire."

I knew he'd come. My heart was beating so I had to hold it hard with my free hand and I had to bite my lips to make them limber. But, honest to God, when I heard him – clear and distinct right in my ear – I thought I was going to faint. For at last I'd got the Voice!

"What's this about finding a key?" he said gruff and sharp.

"Am I speaking to Mr Cokesbury?"

"You are. Who is it?"

"No one you know, sir. I've just come in from Philadelphia and on the Pullman step I found a package which seems to have a key in it. I noticed that it was addressed to you and I looked you up in the telephone book and am phoning now from Jersey City."

He was very cordial then. His voice was the same deep, pleasant one he'd used to Sylvia.

"That's very kind of you and very thoughtful. I can't thank you enough. The package was given to the Pullman conductor and he's evidently dropped it."

"Then shall I give it to the Pullman conductor now?"

"If you'll be so kind. My servant's gone over there to get it. Just hand it to the conductor – a tall, thin man, whose name is Sands."

"I'll do it right off. Ain't it lucky I found it?"

"Very. I'm deeply grateful. It would have put me to the greatest inconvenience if it had been lost. I'd like to know to whom I'm indebted."

"Oh, that don't need to bother you. I'm just a passenger traveling down on the train. Awful glad I could be of any service. Goodbye."

I waited a minute till I got my heart quieted down, then took a call for Babbitts' paper. Luck was with me all round that night, for he was there. I couldn't tell him everything – I was afraid – but I told him enough to show him I'd landed Cokesbury and he answered to come across to town and he'd meet me at the Ferry. I caught a boat as it pulled out of the slip and at the other side he was waiting for me.

"Come on," he said, putting his hand through my arm and walking quick for the street, "I got a taxi here. We'll charge it up to the defense."

I got in, supposing he was going to take me somewhere to dinner, but he wasn't. When I heard where we were bound

I was sort of scared – it was to Wilbur Whitney's house, Jack Reddy's lawyer.

"He's expecting us," Babbitts explained. "I called him up right after I'd heard from you. You see, Kiddo, we don't want to lose a minute for we can't stop Cokesbury going unless we got something to stop him for."

Mr Whitney's house was a big, grand mansion just off Fifth Avenue. A butler let us in and without waiting to hear who we were showed us into a room with lights in bunches along the walls, small spindly gold chairs and sofas, and a floor that shone like glass between elegant soft rugs. There was some class to it and Babbitts and I looked like a pair of tramps sitting side by side on two of the gold chairs. I was nervous but Babbitts kept me up, telling me Mr Whitney was a delightful gentleman and was going to jump for all I had to say. Then we heard steps coming down the stairs – two people – and I swallowed hard being dry in the mouth, what with fright and having had no supper.

Mr Whitney was the real thing. He was a big man, with a square jaw and eyes deep in under thick eyebrows. He spoke so easy and friendly that you forgot how awful sharp and keen those eyes were and how they watched you all the time you were talking. A young man came with him – a real classy chap – that he introduced to me as his son, George.

They couldn't have acted more cordial to me and Babbitts if we'd been the King and Queen of Spain. When they sat down and asked me to tell them what I knew I loosened up quite natural and told the whole story.

The young man sat sideways on the gold sofa, smoking a cigarette and looking into the air with his eyes narrowed up as if he was spying at something a long ways off. Mr Whitney was sort of slouched down in an easy chair with his hands – white as a woman's – hanging over the arms. Now and then he'd ask me a question – always begging my pardon for interrupting – and though they were so calm and quiet I could feel, as if it was in the air, that they were concentrated close on every word I said.

When I got through Mr Whitney said, very cheerful, as if I'd been telling some yarn in a story book:

"That's very interesting, Miss Morganthau, and very well told. Quite a narrative gift, eh George?" and he looked at his son.

"First-class story," said George, and as careless as you please flicked off his cigarette ashes on the rug.

Mr Whitney leaned forward clasping his big white hands between his knees and looking into my face, half-smiling but with something terrible keen behind the smile.

"How can you be so sure of the voice, Miss Morganthau? I don't know whether on the phone I could recognize the voice of my own son here."

"You get that way in my work," I answered. "Your ear gets trained for voices."

"You're absolutely certain," said young Mr Whitney, "that in that message you overheard, the man spoke of coming to the meeting place in his auto?"

"Yes, sir, I'm certain he said that."

He turned and looked at his father.

"And investigations have shown he had no auto, he telephoned to no other garage for one, he kept no horses, and to get there on his own feet, would have had to walk through bad country roads a distance of twenty-five miles."

"Um," answered old Mr Whitney as if he wasn't interested and then he said to me: "In this message you heard today no suggestion was given of what that key was the key of?"

"No, sir. The man just said it was important and Mr Cokesbury'd had the house upside down looking for it."

"Um," said Mr Whitney again. "I rather fancy, Miss Morganthau, you've done us a double service; in hunting for a voice, you've stumbled on a key."

Young Mr Whitney laughed.

"It's probably the key of his front door."

"Perhaps," said his father, and looked down on the carpet as if he was thinking.

Then Babbitts spoke up:

"Don't criminals, no matter how careful they are, often overlook some small clew that maybe is the very thing that gives them away?"

"Often," said Mr Whitney. "In most crimes there's a curious lack of attention to detail. The large matters are well conceived and skillfully carried out. And then some minor point is neglected, sometimes forgotten, sometimes not realized for its proper value."

He got up and shook himself like a big bear and we all rose to our feet. I was feeling pretty fine, not only the relief of having delivered the goods, but proud of myself for getting through the interview so well. Mr Whitney added to it by saying:

"You're a pretty smart girl, Miss Morganthau. *You* don't know and *I* don't know yet the full value of the work you've done for me and my client. But whatever the outcome may be you've shown an energy and keenness of mind that is as surprising as it is unusual."

I just swelled up with importance and didn't know what to say. Behind Mr Whitney I could see Babbitts' face, all beaming and grinning, and I was so glad he was there to hear. And then – just when I was at the top-notch of my pride – Mr George Whitney, who'd been silent for a while, said suddenly:

"If you don't mind me asking, Miss Morganthau, I'd like to know what lucky chance made you listen in to that conversation between Miss Hesketh and the Unknown Man."

Believe me I came down to earth with a thud. How could I tell them? Say I listened to everything in the hope of hearing Jack Reddy talking to Sylvia. I looked down on the floor, feeling my cheeks getting as red as fire.

"Go ahead," said Babbitts. "Don't be afraid to say anything."

"We're as close here as the confessional," said old Mr Whitney, smiling at me like a father.

I had to say something and took what seemed to me the most natural.

"I'd heard Miss Hesketh was a great one for jollying up the men and I wanted to hear how she did it."

And they all – that means Babbitts, too – just burst out and *roared*.

"Good for you, Miss Morganthau," said Mr Whitney, and he put his hand on my shoulder and gave it a shake. "Only I'll bet a hat you didn't need any teaching."

He turned to his son and said something about "the car being there," and then back to me:

"Now for a few days, Miss Morganthau, I'll expect you to be off duty in a place accessible by telephone."

"Off duty!" I exclaimed. "How can I do that?"

He smiled in his easy way and said:

"We'll attend to that, don't you worry about it. Go home and stay there till you get a call from me. If anyone asks what's the matter say you're ill and laid off for a few days. Don't bother about reporting at the office; that'll be arranged. And I need hardly tell you not to speak a word of what you've discovered or of this interview here tonight."

"She won't," said Babbitts. "I'll go bail for that."

He gave Mr George Whitney Mrs Galway's telephone number and then we shook hands all round. I was just wondering what was the quickest way to the Ferry when Mr Whitney said:

"The motor's waiting for you and I'm sure Mr Babbitts will escort you to the boat. Goodnight and remember – hold yourself ready for a call to come to my office."

The car waiting outside was Mr Whitney's own. Gee, it was swell! A footwarmer and a fur rug and a clock and a bottle of salts for me to sniff at. I didn't tell Babbitts I'd had no dinner, for I was ashamed to have the chauffeur stop at the kind of joints we patronize, and so I bore the ache in my insides and tried to believe the footwarmer and the salts made up for it.

XIII

At noon the next day – Friday – I was called to Mrs Galway's phone. It was Mr George Whitney telling me to come over to the city at once. I wasn't to bother about addresses or finding my way. I'd be met at the Ferry and taken to Mr Whitney's office in Broad Street – all I was to do was to say nothing to anybody and come.

I did both.

At the Ferry a fine-looking chap came up to me, with his hat in his hand, and asked me if I was Miss Morganthau. For a moment I was uneasy, thinking maybe he was a masher, when he turned to a kind-faced elderly woman beside him and said:

"This is Mrs Cresset, who's come over on the boat with you and is going to Mr Whitney's office, too."

Then I knew it was all right and we three got into a taxi. On the way across to Broad Street he told us what we were to do. It was nothing much. All Mr Whitney wanted of us was that we'd sit in the inner office and listen to some gentleman talking in the next room. If we heard the voice I'd got on the wire and Mrs Cresset had heard the night of the murder we were to say nothing, but sit perfectly still till we were called.

"If you recognize the voice make no sign or sound. All we ask of you is, if you're not certain of the identification, to say so."

The office was a great big place, rooms opening out of rooms, and a switchboard with a girl at it, dressed very neat and not noticing us as we passed her. Mr George Whitney met us and took us into a room furnished fine with leather armchairs and books all up the walls and a wide window looking out over the roofs and skyscrapers. There was a door at one side, and this he opened a crack and told Mrs Cresset to sit down close to it with me opposite. He cautioned us to be quiet and not to move or even whisper till we were called.

We sat there for a while with nothing happening. We could hear voices, and now and then people walking and doors shutting, and once a bell tinkled far off in the distance. Then suddenly I heard someone – Mr George Whitney, I think – say, "Show him in, the private office," and heavy steps coming up the passage, past our door and into the next room, then old Mr Whitney's voice, very loud and cheerful.

"Ah, Mr Cokesbury, this is truly kind of you. I have to apologize for taking up your time, just as you're leaving, too, but we hoped you might help us in some minor points of this curious case."

The voice that answered was Cokesbury's; I knew it well now. At the sound of it Mrs Cresset gave a start and leaned forward, her ear close to the door.

He was as cordial and hearty as if he was at a pink tea.

"Only too glad to be of service, Mr Whitney. If I had thought I could be of any help I would have offered before. Fortunately for me – as you probably know – I was held up in my place on the day of the murder. If my car had been in working order I suppose I'd have been quite a prominent figure in the case by now."

He laughed out, a deep, rich sort of laugh, and it made my flesh creep to think he could do it with that girl's death at his door.

The talk went on for a bit, back and forth between them, Mr Whitney asking him some questions about the roads, the distances, and Miss Hesketh's friends; he answering as calm and fluent as if he'd hardly known her at all.

In the middle of it the clerk who had met us at the Ferry came softly in, and without a word, beckoned us to follow him through a door that led into another room. We rose up as stealthily as burglars and stole across the carpet without making so much as a creak or a rustle. When we were in he shut the door, told us to wait there, and left us. We sat, afraid to speak, staring at each other and wondering what was going to happen next. In a few minutes the door opened and Mr Whitney came in.

"Well?" he said, turning to me, "are you as sure as you were over the phone?"

"Certain," I answered. "It's the man."

He looked at Mrs Cresset.

"How about you, Mrs Cresset? Remember, a mistake in a matter like this is a pretty serious thing."

Mrs Cresset was as sure as I was.

"I couldn't tell the man from Adam," she said, "but I knew his voice the minute I heard it."

"Very well. Now I want you to come into the private office. Don't be frightened; nothing disagreeable's going to happen. All you have to do is to answer simply and truthfully any questions I may put to you. Come along."

We followed him up the passage to the room where he'd been talking. Sitting in a large chair by the desk was the man I'd seen that day in the woods with Sylvia Hesketh. He didn't look so robust and hearty as he had then; his skin was paler and his forehead lined; but I noticed his large coarse hands with the hair on them – a murderer's hands – *they* were the same.

When he saw us, walking in solemn behind Mr Whitney, his face changed. It's hard to explain how it looked, but it was as if the muscles tightened up and the eyes got a fixed startled expression like you see in the eyes of an animal you've come on sudden and scared. He rose to his feet and I saw one of his hands close till the knuckles turned white. Mr George

Whitney, who was standing near by, watched him like a cat watching a mouse.

Old Mr Whitney spoke up as genial as if he was introducing us at a party.

"These ladies, Mr Cokesbury, come from Longwood and its vicinity. Miss Morganthau is one of the operators in the Telephone Exchange, and Mrs Cresset you've met before, I think, one night at Cresset's Farm."

Mrs Cresset bowed very polite and made as if she was going to shake hands. But Cokesbury didn't meet her half or a quarter way. He turned to the men and – I guess he did it without knowing – looked like lightning from one to the other – a sort of wild glance. They never took their eyes off him, and there was something awful about their stare, for all both of them were behaving so pleasant. Under that stare he got as white as a sheet, but he tried to put up a bluff.

"Cresset," he said, "Cresset? There's some mistake. I never saw her before in my life."

"That's quite true," said Mr Whitney, "you didn't see her nor she you. If you remember it was very dark. But you spoke to her and she's willing to swear that yours was the voice she heard. Aren't you, Mrs Cresset?"

"Yes, sir," said Mrs Cresset, as solid and sure as the Bartholdi statue. "This is the gentleman that asked me the way that night. I'd know his voice among a thousand."

"What night?" said Cokesbury. "I don't know what she's talking about."

It was pitiful to see him trying to keep it up with his face gray and his hands trembling.

Mr Whitney went on as if he didn't notice anything.

"And Miss Morganthau here is also ready to swear to your voice as the one she overheard on the phone Saturday, November the twentieth, in a conversation with the late Miss Hesketh – a message you've probably seen a good deal about in the papers."

I saw one of those big, hairy hands make a grip at the back of the armchair. I thought he was going to fall and couldn't take my eyes off him till Mr Whitney turned to me and said in that bland society way:

"Perhaps you'll be so good, Miss Morganthau, as to tell Mr Cokesbury of your efforts during the past week to get him on the phone."

I told him the whole thing and ended up with the story of how I fooled him about the key. And, honest to God, though I thought I was talking to a murderer, I was sorry for him.

All the life seemed to leave him and he got as haggard as an old man, with his lips shaking and the perspiration in beads on his forehead. When I got through he suddenly gave a sort of groan, dropped back into his chair and put his hands over his face. I was glad it was hidden, and I was glad when Mr Whitney turned to me and Mrs Cresset and said quick and commanding:

"That'll do. You can go into the other room. Ring the bell, George."

We huddled out into the passage where we met that spry clerk coming up on the jump. He went into the office and shut the door, and we could hear a murmur of voices, we standing up against the wall not knowing what to do next.

Presently the clerk came out again, rounded us up and sent us into the room down the hall where Mr Whitney had talked to us. He told us to wait there for a minute, then lit out as if he was in a great hurry. We stood stiff in the middle of the floor, expecting to hear the tramp of policemen and then Cokesbury being dragged off to jail. But it was all very still. I never supposed when you caught a criminal the proceedings would be so natural and dignified.

After a while the clerk came back. He said Mr Whitney'd sent us his thanks for our kindness in coming – I never saw people waste so many words on politeness – and hoped we'd excuse him from thanking us in person, but he was just now very busy. He warned us not to say a word to anyone of what had transpired, and then a boy coming to the door and saying, "It's here," he told us a taxi was waiting below to take us to the Ferry.

If we couldn't talk to anyone else we could to each other and I guess we did more gabbing going down in the taxi and across in the boat than Mrs Cresset had done for years. She told me about the night when Cokesbury had come to her house. It was wonderful to see how luck was with him – the way it sometimes is with sinners. Usually at that hour she was round in the kitchen and when he knocked would have opened the door and seen his face in the lamplight. But she'd gone upstairs early as her little daughter had a cold.

To go back over the small things that happened would make you sure some evil power was protecting him. That morning the little girl's cold wasn't bad and she'd gone to school as usual. But at the schoolhouse she heard that the dancing bear – the one I saw in Longwood which had been performing along the pike on its way back to Bloomington – had been at Jaycock's farm and might be round by Cresset's that afternoon. Like all children, she was crazy about the bear, and after school hours she and a chum slipped off and stood around in the damp, waiting. But the bear did not show up and when she came home, crying with disappointment, the cold was heavy on her. Her mother bundled her off to bed and went up early to sit with her. Only for that, Cokesbury would probably have been landed in jail weeks before, the State saved money and two innocent men saved shame and suffering.

"That's the way it is with the Devil's own," I said. "I guess he takes care of them for a while; jollies them along the downward path."

"It looks like that was the case," said Mrs Cresset, her kind, rosy face very solemn. "But the power of evil gets broke in the end. 'Murder will out' – that's true if anything is. Think of that man feeling so safe and every hour the cords tightening round him."

"And *we* did it," said I, awful proud. "We found the cords and then pulled on them."

"We did," says she. "I never thought to be the one to put a fellow-creature behind bars, but I have and my conscience tells me I've done right."

My, but we both felt chesty!

The next morning Babbitts phoned me to say he'd be over Sunday evening. The information of "Our Suspect" would be given to the press Sunday morning for the Monday papers and after it was in he'd come across and tell me about it.

Mr Whitney had arranged for me not to go back to work till Tuesday and though I suppose the rest was good for me, the strain of waiting wore on me something dreadful. I kept wondering how Cokesbury had done it, and how he was going to explain this and account for that. Most of Sunday I lay on the bed trying to read a novel, but a great deal more interested in the hands of the clock than I was in the printed pages.

When it began to darken up for evening I told Mrs Galway I was expecting a gentleman caller and asked for the loan of the parlor. She's a great one for love affairs and it always discouraged her that I had no regular company. Now she thought I'd got a steady at last and wanted to lend me her cameo pin, and decked up the parlor as if the minister was coming to call, with the hand-painted leather cushion and the punch-work tablecloth.

Long before Babbitts was due I was sitting by the stove, burning bright and clear, with the drop light throwing a glow over the center table. Upstairs I could hear Mrs Galway tramping round as she went to bed, which was considerate of her as she was something of a night bird. When I heard his knock at the side door, I gave a sort of squeal of excitement and ran to let him in.

"Well?" I said, grabbing his arm, too worked up to say goodevening, "has he confessed?"

"Yes," he said, "he has and he's told an uncommon queer story."

"He killed her?"

"That's the queerest part of it," said Babbitts slowly, "he didn't."

XIV

Now I don't believe if I gave you twenty guesses you'd know what I did when I heard those words – burst out crying.

It wasn't because I wanted Cokesbury to be executed; it wasn't because I wanted the reward; it wasn't even that I was so crazy to have Jack Reddy exonerated – it was just because I was so disappointed – so *foiled* – that I couldn't seem to bear it.

I cried so hard I didn't know what I was doing, and I suppose that's the reason I leaned on Babbitts' shoulder, it being the nearest thing handy. He brought me to my senses, patting me on the arm and saying sort of soothing as if he was comforting a child who'd broken her doll:

"There, there – don't cry – it'll be all right soon. We'll get the right man. Don't take it to heart that way."

Then I began to laugh, for it did seem so comical – me crying because Cokesbury wasn't a murderer, and Babbitts telling me not to take it to heart as if I'd been disappointed in not seeing the electrocution. The laughter and tears got mixed up together and I don't know where I'd have landed if I hadn't seen he was getting frightened and wanted to call Mrs Galway. That pulled me up, and I got a hold on myself. In a few minutes we were sitting side by side in front of the stove, the storm over, all but a little hiccupy kind of sob, that came upon me unexpected at intervals.

For the next hour we sat there without moving while Babbitts told me Cokesbury's story.

I'll put down what he said as near his words as I can remember it. The way he told it was better than any of the newspaper accounts, even his, though he got a raise of salary for the way he'd handled it:

"Cokesbury says he didn't kill Sylvia Hesketh and I believe him and so do the Whitneys. Besides the corroborative evidence is absolutely convincing. He's not a murderer but he's a coward – no good at all – and that explains why he didn't come out after the crime and tell what he knew. Instead he got in a panic, lost what little nerve he had, and was skipping out to Europe when you nabbed him.

"He was in love with Sylvia Hesketh, if you call that sort of thing love. Anyway, instead of being simply what you might describe as a beau of hers, he was mad about her. I fancy even she, poor girl, didn't realize the passion she'd kindled, but was like a child playing with a dynamite bomb. It appears she saw more of him than anybody guessed. After the first flirtation at Bar Harbor, he came down to Cokesbury Lodge nearly every Sunday and used to meet her in the woods and on the side roads, and make dates with her for theaters and concerts in town. He kept it quiet for he knew without being told that the Doctor wouldn't stand for it. His hope was that, willful and unstable as he knew her to be, he'd eventually win her by his persistence and devotion.

"It was one of those situations that may end in nothing or may end as this one did in a tragedy. The girl was foolhardy and flirtatious; the man infatuated. Very quickly he got on to the fact that he was not the only victim of her beauty and her wiles. He watched and questioned and found out about the other men. Of them he soon saw that Reddy was the favored one and a deadly jealousy seized him, for Reddy might have attracted any woman.

"When he tried to find out from her how she stood with Reddy he could get no satisfaction. She'd tell him one thing one day and another the next. She kept them all guessing, but it didn't mean to any of the others what it meant to Cokesbury. All through October he spied and queried, and learnt that she was meeting Reddy in his car and going off for long jaunts with him. He says he was half mad with jealousy and fear, but he hid it from her.

"That's the way things were when he sent the phone message that you caught. You sized him up just right. When she told him she had a date that was a secret, he got a premonition of the truth, the way a man does when his reason is under the dominion of his emotions. He felt certain she was going off with Reddy, and the brakes that he'd kept down till then were lifted. He determined he'd find out and if it was true stop them if the skies fell.

"And now here comes the queer part of the story. If anybody'd guessed it a lot of things that were dark would have been as clear as daylight. He *did* keep the date you heard him make on the phone."

"How could he? He had no car, or horse, or anything."

"Only part of that's true – he had no car, or horse, but he *did* have something."

"What?"

"An aeroplane."

I fell back staring at him.

"An aeroplane – in Cokesbury Lodge?"

"In the garage there. *That's* why he wouldn't rent the house; *that's* why he kept going down over Sunday all summer. The year he was in France he'd done a lot of flying and was fascinated by it. Before he left there he was an expert aviator, but his wife hated it and it was one of their grounds of dissension. After she died he had a machine brought down in sections, set it up himself, and kept it in the garage. Not a soul knew it. He only flew at night for he wanted it kept a secret."

"Why – what for?"

"Because – here's the best thing I've heard about him – he carried a heavy life insurance policy secured to his children. Cokesbury's not a rich man, though he has a good business, and if he died his children would have had to live on what their mother left them, which wasn't much. If it was known that he was aviating the policy would have been invalidated, so he indulged his secret passion at night. The isolated position of the house made it easy to escape detection and his machine was equipped with a very silent muffler. No one had a glimmering of it, not even Sylvia.

"The phone message you heard was sent from the station at Jersey City and when he sent it he *did* intend coming to Mapleshade in his motor. When he got to Azalea and found the car unmended in the garage he flew into a rage, as he thought his plans were blocked. Alone in the Lodge, ravaged by jealousy, he lost all caution and decided to take out the aeroplane.

"You remember that there was a moon that night, but that in the evening the skies were clouded and the air breathless. The darkness and the weather were on his side and he came down in a field about ten minutes walk from the house, closing the cut-out as he descended. He was early and hid himself among some trees where he could watch the front door. He says it was while he was waiting there for her that the idea came to him of frustrating an elopement by carrying her off.

"He was laying round in his mind how he would get the truth from her, when he saw her come out and gave a low whistle. She heard it and came toward him. It was not till she was close to him and he could see the outlines of her figure through the dark, that he made out a bag in her hand. *Then* he knew for certain she was going and decided on his course.

"In all his other dealings with her he had found her subtle and evasive. Now, perhaps because for the first time in her life she had decided on a positive action, she went straight to the point. Without any preamble she told him what she was going to do and that within a half-hour Reddy would be waiting for her in the Lane.

"He showed no anger or surprise, apparently accepting the situation in the most friendly spirit. He says he thought she was relieved, having expected a scene with him. When he had disarmed her of her suspicions, he told her of the airship and asked her if she wouldn't like to come up for a spin before Reddy arrived. They had over half an hour and he could take her for a short flight and would bring her down in ten or fifteen minutes.

"Everybody agrees that she was a bold, venturesome girl, and the idea appealed to her, as she had never been up. They walked quickly through the fields and bit of woodland to the aeroplane. She was in high spirits as she tucked herself in; he could hear her laughter as he took his seat, and then, closing the cut-out, they soared up.

"They rose high – about two thousand feet, he thought – and then he headed East. They were winging their way over Cokesbury Lodge on toward the hills in the distance when Reddy must have sighted the lights of Longwood as he came down the Firehill Road.

"Cokesbury swears he had no intention of kidnapping her. He says he had no definite idea of where he was going, that his plan was simply to get her away from Reddy and put an end to the marriage. Personally, I don't believe him. I think he had a perfectly clear idea of carrying her off to Cokesbury Lodge, and that his chivalrous scheme was to put her into such a compromising position she would be willing to marry him. Maybe I'm wrong – I don't know. Anyway, he very soon saw you can't abduct a high-spirited, hot-tempered girl against her will.

"After about fifteen or twenty minutes he was conscious of her getting uneasy and speaking to him – words that he couldn't hear but that he knew to be at first startled questions, then angry commands. He shouted replies, but the great machine kept steadily on its way, neither turning nor dipping downward. Then she realized and broke into a fury, turning upon him in the dark, putting her face close to his and screaming for him to bring her down. The noise made it impossible to argue with her, and fearful of what she might do, he held her off with his elbow, the delicately balanced machine swaying as she seized his arm and shook it, lunging up against him, her cries of rage rising above the thunder of the screw.

"Can't you imagine it? The big ship sailing through the night with the lights of farms and little towns sliding by far below, and above the sky muffled deep in black clouds. Poised between them the man and woman, each gripped by a different passion – suspended there like two naked souls in a sort of elemental battle of the sexes.

"He admits he was scared and if he could have spoken to her would have pacified her with all sorts of assurances. But speech was out of the question, and when she made a sudden lunge across him for the wheel he realized she would kill them both if he didn't bring her to earth. Throwing her back with a blow of his elbow, he yelled that he was coming down and as she felt the machine begin its glancing, downward glide she fell back into her place, suddenly quiet, then leaned forward scanning the country below them.

"A momentary break of the clouds let a little light spill through and by this he saw a bare, bold landscape darkened by woods, and with the gleam of a large body of water to the right, showing against the blackness like polished steel. He made a landing in an open space, an uncultivated field with a hillock in the center covered with grass and surrounded by trees. The water had drained off this and it was quite dry.

"She was hardly out on the ground and he was preparing for an explanation when to his surprise she curtly told him to follow her and led the way along a ridge that skirted the lake. This, too, was dry, a fact curiously in his favor, for their feet left no tracks, the grass closing on the trail they swept through it. She did not address him again till, the dim shape of a house appearing, he asked her if she was going there and she answered in the same, curt way: Yes; she was cold. A wharf jutted out in front of the house and in stepping from the grass to the planks he made a motion to help her, but she started away from him as if he was a snake, making two or three steps into the liquid mud that ran up to the wharf's edge. It was then he thought she dropped the glove. Once again on the planks she took a key from her purse, fitted it in the lock and opened the door.

"The room was pitch dark and Cokesbury stood in the doorway while she went in. She moved about as if she was accustomed to the place, lit a lamp, set a match to the fire already laid and gave him a copper kettle to fill with water from the lake. When he came back with it the table was set out with tea things and the fire was leaping up the chimney. She hung the kettle on a crane, swung it over the flames and then, turning to him, said:

"'Do you know where you are?' He said he didn't and she answered: 'You're in Jack Reddy's bungalow at Hochalaga Lake, the place where I've spent the happiest days of my life.'

"He looked at her in amazement and she smiled scornfully back at him. 'You fool!' she said, 'to think you could come blundering in and stop me from marrying the only man of all of you who's worth a heartbeat.'

"She made tea and then motioned him to sit down by the table, taking a seat at the other side. Facing each other in the lamplight they had a conversation that put an end to all his dreams. For the first time in his acquaintance with her he thought she spoke frankly. She told him of her friendship with Reddy from the start, and how the Doctor's senseless opposition had fanned a boy-and-girl flirtation into a passionate love affair.

"When the quarrels began at Mapleshade they found that they could meet without fear of detection at the Lake, she going out there in her car and he in his. She had her own key and often, during the autumn, she had gone to the bungalow in the morning, Reddy had joined her and they had spent the day together, canoeing and fishing on the lake, cooking a picnic meal over the fire, and driving home in the afternoon, the racer towing her car till they came to the turnpike.

"Cokesbury says he thinks at first it was only the spirit of romance and adventure which made her do such a rash thing, but that in the end Reddy's devotion and chivalrous attitude made a deep impression on her and she came as near loving him as she could any man. He says there is no doubt that the meetings were perfectly innocent and that Reddy had behaved from the start as a gentleman.

"'Whether she really loved him or not,' he said, 'he'd taught her to respect him.'

"They talked for over an hour, taking the tea she had made and Cokesbury smoking a cigar. He remembered leaving the butt in the saucer of his cup. It was half-past eight when they rose to go. Sylvia put out the lamp but the fire was still burning and the tea things were left on the table. Cokesbury says he promised to take her home, that he saw his case was hopeless, and he'd made up his mind to have done with her forever.

"The sky was clouded over and it was as dark as a pocket when they went back to the aeroplane. He had to direct the machine by guesswork, the country black below him and the sky black above. He swears that he intended to take her back to Mapleshade, and I believe him. No man – not even a bad egg like Cokesbury – wants to run away with a woman who hands out the line of talk that girl had in the bungalow.

"Anyway, we've only his word for the statement that he completely lost his bearings. He could see no lights and after making an exploratory circle, realized he hadn't the slightest idea which way to go. To make matters worse, he could hear from shouted remarks of hers that her suspicions were on the alert and that she was ready to flare up again. By this time there wasn't much of the lover left in him. According to his own words he was as anxious to get her home again as she was to be there. With his head clear and his blood cold he did not relish a second flight with a woman fighting like a wildcat.

"This was the situation – she, angry and disbelieving; he, scared and unable to conciliate her – when the twinkle of a light caught his eye and he decided to come down and ask his way. They dropped into a stretch of grass land among fields, with the light shining some way off through a screen of trees. Farther away, just a spark, he saw another light. He told her to wait while he went to inquire, and walked off toward the one that was nearest.

"It was Cresset's Farm. There he had the interview with Mrs Cresset, telling her he had an auto in order to explain his presence. When he went back he found that Sylvia had disappeared. At first he didn't know what to do, realizing that if the story of their flight got abroad, there would be the devil to pay. He was certain she had disbelieved him and had taken the opportunity to get away from him. She was either hiding or had gone for the second light. This being the most plausible, he walked toward it – quite a distance across fields and through woods – and brought up at a ramshackle roadhouse – the Wayside Arbor.

"He stole round from the back to a side window and there, through a crack in the shutter, looked in and saw Sylvia talking to Hines. He says he stayed there for some minutes, afraid if he went in after her she would make a scene and start a scandal. Then his eyes fell on the telephone booth and he felt sure she had telephoned either to her own home or to Reddy. Her air of waiting – she was sitting by the stove with her feet on its lower edge – confirmed him in this and he decided to let her alone.

"He went back to the aeroplane, wondering what would be the outcome of the whole crazy escapade. He says he felt confident of her cleverness to hush the thing up, but he was uneasy. His discomfort wasn't lessened when he found that she had left her bag in the machine, and on his way home one of the things that preoccupied him was thinking up the best way of getting the bag back to her.

"Monday morning he went to town in a state of suspense. If she should tell there was no knowing what might happen and he was on the alert for a visit from the Doctor or even Reddy. But the day passed without any sign of trouble, and he was just calming down, thinking she had either found Reddy and gone with him or invented some story to quiet the Mapleshade people, when he read of the murder in the evening paper.

"*Then*, you better believe he was frightened. He knew the bag was hidden in his room at the Lodge and that as far as he could tell, not a soul had seen the airship. As to Mrs Cresset, he felt safe for she couldn't possibly have made out a feature in the darkness."

"But," I cried out, "why if he hadn't done it—"

"That's all right," Babbitts interrupted. "He hadn't done it, but I tell you he was a coward. He was in a sweat for fear of being suspected, of being pulled in as a witness, of his reputation, his business, his position. He wanted to keep out of it at any cost."

"What a cur!" I said.

"Oh, he's that and more, and he's ready to admit it himself. But it wasn't as smooth sailing as he thought it would be. After the inquest he read of the overheard phone message and that brought him up with a jolt. He got in a state of terror, realizing too late that his silence was more incriminating than any confession.

"Every day his fears grew worse. He wouldn't answer any phone calls, faking up reasons to his clerks and his servants. Finally it got on his nerves so he couldn't stand it and he made ready to skip to Europe. The key was what tripped him up. Do you remember Mr Whitney saying how criminals overlooked important details? Well, what he overlooked was the key of the garage. In his preoccupation on Monday morning he had put it in the pocket of the raincoat he was accustomed to leave in the auto and had simply forgotten it. Then when he went to pack his things he couldn't find it, hunted in a nervous frenzy and finally had his man telephone over to Miner's place. You and the key were the combination that beat him."

"But Jack Reddy?" I said. "Was he going to slink off and let him be tried for the murder when he could have cleared it all up?"

"He *says* not and I guess the fellow's not as yellow as to have stood by and let an innocent man go to his death. He says there wasn't enough evidence to convict Reddy and if things had gone badly he would have come out and told what he knew. And I think that's true – anyway, we'll give him the benefit of the doubt."

"How can you be so sure? How do you know he's *not* the murderer after all?"

"Oh, there's no doubt. Everything fits in too well. The police were out at Cokesbury Lodge on Saturday and saw the aeroplane and found Miss Hesketh's bag. Both the Whitneys – father and son, who've had a vast experience in this sort of case – say there's no question of his innocence."

We sat silent for a spell, looking at the stove, then I said:

"We're back just where we were in the beginning."

Babbitts leaned forward and shook down some ashes.

"The case is, but we're not," he said.

"How do you make that out?" I asked.

"Six weeks ago we didn't know each other and now we're friends."

"That's so," I said, and we both sat staring thoughtfully at the red eye of the stove.

XV

Cokesbury's story made a great sensation. Even if it didn't bring us any nearer to finding the murderer, it explained the mystery of Sylvia's movements up to the time she appeared in the Wayside Arbor, and it cleared Jack Reddy. Babbitts told me that the Whitneys were doing some legal stunts – I won't tell what they were for I'd never get them straight – to have him liberated, and that they would soon issue a statement to the press.

When it came out everybody saw why he had said such contradictory things about those seven hours on the road.

Babbitts and I had guessed right when we thought he was holding something back and when I heard why I was grateful to him. Yes, grateful, that's the word. And I'll tell you why I use it. He was my hero and he stayed a hero, didn't fall down and disappoint me, but made me know there were people in the world who could stick to their standard no matter *what* happened. Don't you think that's a thing to be grateful for?

The reason he didn't tell was to protect the memory of that poor dead girl, who couldn't rise up and protect herself. He knew what wicked lies would be told and believed and he was going to shield her in death as he would have in life.

That night after he had searched the roads, he suddenly thought that in some wild freak she had gone to the bungalow in her own car and phoned him from there. As soon as the idea entered his head he went out to the lake. One glance showed him someone had been there before him – the room was warm, the fire still smouldering on the hearth. He lit the light and saw the two teacups and the cigar butt on the saucer. He examined the doors and windows and found that they were locked and there was no sign of anyone having broken in. The only person beside himself who had a key to the bungalow was Sylvia.

Then he knew she had been there with another man and one of those fierce rages came on him.

For a spell he was outside himself. He thought of things that never happened, the way people do in a fury – imagined Sylvia sending him the phone message with the other man standing by and laughing. He tore her letters out of the desk and threw them in the fire and smashed the tea things against the side of the house. He was half crazy, thinking himself fooled and made a mock of by the woman he had loved.

When his rage quieted down he sat brooding over the fire for a long time. It was moonlight when he left, bright enough for him to fill the tank. He had never thought about any inquiries for the missing drum till at the inquest the question of the gasoline was sprung on him. Then he lied, feeling certain that no one would ever go out to the lake. It was his intention to go there himself, hide the drum and clear out the cottage, but he put it off, hating to go near the place. If Pat Donahue hadn't gone there to fish through the ice – a thing no one would have dreamed of – the secret of the bungalow would never have been discovered.

One of the features of the case that he couldn't understand and that he spent the days in jail speculating about, was how she had reached the lake. The mud showed the tracks of only one auto, his own. He could find no solution to this mystery and he could speak to no one about it. Whatever happened to him, he had made up his mind he would never give her up to the evil-minded and evil-tongued who would blacken and tear to pieces all that was left of her.

He was liberated, and, believe me, Longwood rejoiced. It was as if a king who had been banished had come back to his throne.

I don't think he was home two days when he telephoned in asking me if he could come to see me and thank me for what I'd done. Wasn't that like him? Most men would have been so glad to get out of jail they'd have forgotten the hello girl who'd helped to free them, but not Jack Reddy.

He came in the late afternoon, at the time I got off. I'll never forget it. Katie Reilly was at the switchboard and I was standing at the window, watching, when I saw the two lights of the gray racer coming down the street.

I ran and opened the door – I wasn't bashful a bit – and when I saw him I gave a little cry, for he looked so changed, pale and haggard and older, a good many years older. But his smile was the same, and so was the kind, honest look of his face. Before he said a word he just held out his hand and mine went into it and I felt the clasp of his fingers warm and strong. And – strange it is, but true – I wasn't any more like the girl who used to tremble at the mere sight of him, but was calm and quiet, looking deep and steady into his eyes as if we'd got to be friends, the way a man might be friends with a boy.

"Miss Morganthau," he said, "I've heard what you've done, and I want to thank you."

"You needn't have taken all the trouble to come in from Firehill, Mr Reddy," I answered. "You could have said it over the wire."

"Could I have done this over the wire?" he said, giving my hand a shake and a squeeze. "You know I couldn't. And that's what I wanted to do – take a grip of the hand that helped me out of prison."

I said some fool words about its being nothing and he went on smiling down at me, yet with something grave in his face.

"I want to do more – ask a favor of you. I hope it won't be hard to grant for I've set my heart on it. Can I be your friend?"

"Oh, Mr Reddy," I stammered out, "you make me proud," and suddenly tears came into my eyes. I don't know why unless it was seeing him so changed and hearing him speak so humble to a common guy like me.

"Oh, come now," he said, "don't do anything like that. You'll make me think you don't like the idea."

I sniffed, wanting to kick Katie Reilly, who was gaping round in her chair, and I guess getting mad that way dried up my tears.

"It's your friend I'll be till the end of my life, Mr Reddy," I answered. "And the only thing I'm sorry for is that I didn't get the right man the way I thought I'd done."

"Never mind about that," said he, his face hardening up, "we'll get him yet. Don't let's think of that now. It's the end of your day, isn't it? If you're going home will you let me take you there in my car?"

There was a time when if I'd thought I'd ever ride beside Jack Reddy in that racer I'd have had chills and fever for a week in advance.

But now I sat calm and still beside him as he rode me through Longwood to Mrs Galway's door.

As we swung up the street he talked very kind to me, complimenting me something awful, and saying that if he ever could do anything for me to let him know and he'd do it if it was within the power of man.

"You see, Miss Morganthau," he said as we drew up in front of the Elite, "a man in my position feels pretty grateful to the person who's lifted off him the shadow of disgrace and death."

Up in my room I sat quiet for a long time thinking. The thing that phased me was why I'd changed so, come round to feel that while he was still a grand, strong man, I'd always look up to and do anything for, I'd quit having blind staggers and heart attacks when he came along.

Something had sidetracked me. I didn't know what. All I did know was that two months ago if he'd asked me to be his friend I'd not have known there was such a thing as food in the world. And that evening at half-past seven, being too lazy to go to the Gilt Edge, I was so hungry I had to go down to Mrs Galway and beg the loan of three Uneedas and a hard boiled egg.

It was one evening, not long after, that Anne Hennessey came in to see me. Babbitts was coming that night and Mrs Galway had given up the parlor again and was in bed with a novel and a kerosene lamp. Anne was quite excited, the reason being that Mrs Fowler had given her a present. She took it careful out of a blue velvet case and held it up in the glow of the drop light. It was a diamond cross and the minute I set eyes on it I knew where I'd seen it before.

"Sylvia's," I said, low and sort of awed.

Anne nodded.

"Yes, the one she had on that night. Mrs Fowler said she wanted to give me something that had been hers. I wouldn't have taken anything so handsome but I think the poor lady couldn't bear the sight of it, reminding her of her sorrow as it did."

She moved it about and the stones sparkled like bits of fire in the lamplight. I stretched out my hand and took it, for diamonds tempt me like meat the hungry – that's the Jew in me, I suppose.

"You won't call the King your cousin when you wear this," I said, and I held it against my chest, looking down at the brightness of it.

"That's just where Sylvia had it on," said Anne almost in a whisper, "where the front of her dress crossed. One of the police officers told me."

My mother was a Catholic and it's Catholic I was raised, for though my father was a Jew he loved my mother and let her have her way with me.

"Wouldn't you think," I said, "that when the murderer saw the cross on her it would have stayed his hand?"

"Wouldn't you," said Anne, "but to men as evil as that the cross means nothing. And then out in the dark that way, he probably never saw it."

Babbitts' knock sounding, I handed it back to her and let him in, feeling bashful before Anne, who didn't know how often Mrs Galway was retiring at eight-thirty. She left soon after, saying Mrs Fowler liked her to be round in the evening, which was news to me, as she'd told me that the Fowlers always sat in the sitting-room together, the Doctor reading aloud till Mrs Fowler got sleepy.

After she'd gone, Babbitts and I drew up to the stove, cozy and cheerful, with our feet on the edge of it. We'd come to know each other so well now that we'd other topics beside "the case," but that night we worked around to it, me picking at the box of candy Babbitts had brought and rocking lazily as contented as a child.

Babbitts was still keen for that reward. He said to me:

"You had your fingers on it once, and it's my wish that you'll get your whole hand on it next time."

"What a noble character," said I, "calculating for little Molly to get it all! Where do *you* come in?"

"Oh, don't bother about me," says he. "You've a bad habit of thinking too much where other people come in. You got to quit it – it isn't good business. Now what I want to arrange is for you and me to make an excursion out to the Wayside Arbor some afternoon."

"The Wayside Arbor – what'll we do there?"

"Take a look over the ground. You see, with the process of elimination that's been going on things have narrowed down to the vicinity of the crime. It's my opinion that the murder was not only committed but was planned round there. The police are losing heart and not doing much. As far as I can find out Fowler's detectives – Mills and his crowd – are getting their pay envelopes regular but not getting anything else. Now – just for devilment – let *us* combine our two giant intellects and see what we can see."

"Haven't they gone over every inch of it?"

"They have – with a fine-tooth comb. But that doesn't prevent us going over it and taking our fine-tooth combs along."

"Isn't Hines under surveillance?"

"Good Lord," says he laughing, "*everybody's* under surveillance. There's not one of the suspects but knows he's expected to stay put and is doing it. But who's getting anywhere? There's no reason why we shouldn't go out that way, call on Mrs Cresset, and take a look in at the Wayside Arbor ourselves."

"I'm game," I said, "though I can't see what good it's going to do."

"It'll give us a half-day together," said he. "I don't know how you feel about it but that looks worth while to me."

We made a date for the following Monday, my holiday, just eight weeks from the murder.

The next morning I had a surprise – a kind that hasn't often come my way. It was a letter directed in typewriting with a half-sheet of paper inside it inclosing a fifty-dollar bill. On the paper, also typed, was written:

For Miss Morganthau – A small return for her recent good work in the Hesketh Murder Case.

That was all – no name, no date, no handwriting. I don't know what made me think right off of Mr Whitney, unless it was because there was no one else who knew of what I'd done and could have afforded to send that much. The only other person it could have been was Jack Reddy, and somehow or other, after he'd asked me to be his friend, I felt certain he wouldn't send me money, no matter what I'd done for him. Friends don't pay each other.

I guess there wasn't a more elated person in Longwood that morning than yours truly. I'd had that much before – saved it – but I'd never had it fall out of the sky that way in one beautiful, crisp, new bill.

The Jew and the Irish in me had some tussle, one wanting to salt it down in the bank and the other to blow it in. But that time the Irish had a walk-over, probably because I was limp and weary with all the excitement of the last two months and felt the need of doing something foolish to tone me up. When I thought of the clothes I could buy with it, the Jew just lay down without a murmur and you'd have supposed I was all County Galway if you'd seen me writing a list of things on the back of the envelope. If it'll make you think better of me I'll confess that I wanted to look nice on that trip with Babbitts, the first real jaunt we'd ever taken, for I didn't count those times in New York when we were sleuthing after Cokesbury. Just once in my life I was going to have a real blowout, and I wanted the chap who was taking me to feel he'd some lady with him.

With three of us in the office I fixed things so I got Saturday afternoon and I hiked over to town with that bill burning in my purse like a live coal. And, my it was great spending it! I was cool on the outside, looking haughty at the goods and casting them aside contemptuous on chairs, but inside I was drunk with the feeling of riches.

I bought a one-piece silk dress that fitted me like every measure was mine and a long black plush coat, rich fine plush like satin, that was draped something elegant and fastened in front with a novelty ornament. For a hat I selected a small dark felt, nothing flashy, no trimming, just a rosette at one side. And with the last three dollars a purse, black striped silk, oval shaped with a ribbon to hang it to your wrist.

It was six when I got home, carrying the boxes myself – all but the coat; that I *had* to wear – pretty nearly dead with the weight of them, but not regretting – neither the Jew nor the Irish – one nickel of it.

Midday Monday, when I came down to the parlor where Babbitts was waiting, he put his hand over his eyes like the Indians in front of cigar stores and pretended to stagger.

"What good deed have I ever done," says he, "that I'm allowed to walk the world with such a queen!"

Then I felt certain that to break loose now and again is a healthy change.

XVI

It was a long ride to Cresset's Crossing, first on the main line to the Junction and then just time to make a close connection with the branch line to the Crossing.

It was three when we reached there and started out to walk to Cresset's Farm. There'd been rain the day before and the road was muddy, with water standing here and there in the ruts. The weather was still overcast, the sky covered with clouds, heavy and leaden colored. It was cold, a raw, piercing air, and we walked fast, I – careful of my new dress – picking my steps on the edge of the road and Babbitts tramping along in the mud beside me.

I'd never been up there at that season and I thought it was a gloomy, lonesome spot. The land rolled away with fences creeping across it like gray snakes. Here and there were clumps of woods, purplish against the sky, and between them the brown stretches of plowed land, that in the springtime would be green with the grain. Now, under those dark, low-hanging clouds with the naked trees and the bare, empty fields, it looked forlorn and dreary. It was as still as a picture, not a thing moving, but one man, someways off, walking along the top of a hill. You could see him like a silhouette, going slow, with a bundle on a stick over his shoulder, and a bit of red round his neck. When he got to the highest point he stopped and looked down on the road. He couldn't see us – the trees interfered – and he seemed, as Babbitts said, like the spirit of the landscape –

sort of desolate and lonely, plodding along there, solitary and slow, between the earth and the sky. Then presently even he was gone, disappearing over the brow of the hill.

When we passed the Riven Rock Road and I could see the Firehill one, making a curving line through the country beyond, I had a creepy feeling, thinking of what had happened there eight weeks ago.

"Where's the place?" I said, almost in a whisper, and Babbitts pointed ahead with his cane.

"A little further on, where the bushes grow thick there."

Right along from the station, clumps and bunches of small trees had edged the way like a hedge. After we passed the Riven Rock Road they grew thicker, making a sort of shrubbery higher than our heads. I remembered that just before the murder men had been cutting these for brushwood and even now we passed piles of branches, dry and dead, with little leaves clinging to them like brown rags. Where the Firehill Road ran into the turnpike the growth was tangled and close, almost a small wood.

It wasn't far beyond that Babbitts pointed out the place. There was an edge of shriveled grass and on this she had been found with the branches piled over her. He drew with his cane where she had lain between the trees and the road.

"You can see just how the murderer worked," he said. "He attacked Miss Hesketh here, burst out of the darkness on her and killed her with one blow – you remember there was no sign either about her or the surroundings of a struggle – and almost immediately heard the Doctor's auto horn. We can place that by the scream the Bohemian woman heard."

"Do you think he was there when the Doctor passed?" I asked.

"Of course he was. He hadn't had time to arrange the body. That was done after the Doctor had gone by – done after the moon came out. Reddy said it was as bright as day when he got there. By that brightness the murderer did the work of concealment."

I stepped back into the mud and looked down to where the Firehill Road entered the turnpike a few yards farther on.

"He must have heard Mr Reddy's horn before the car came in sight. By that time he had probably finished and stolen away."

"I don't think so," said Babbitts. "He couldn't have done it without some noise and Reddy, who was listening and watching for Sylvia, was positive there wasn't a sound. That human devil was back among the bushes when Reddy's car came round the turn. And he must have stayed there – afraid to move – watching Reddy, first as he waited, then as he slowly ran back and forth. God, what a situation – one man looking for the woman he loved, her murderer hidden a few yards from him, and between them both her dead body!"

I seemed to see it: the road bathed in moonlight, the murderer huddled down in the black shadow, and Reddy in the car looking now this way and now that, expecting her to come. How terribly still it must have been, not a sound except the rustling of the withered leaves. I could imagine the light from the racer's lamps, shooting out in two long yellow rays, showing every rut and ridge, so that that grim watching face had to draw down lower still in the darkness of the underbrush. Did he know who Reddy was waiting for? What did he feel when the auto moved and one swerve sideways would have sent those yellow rays over the heap of branches on the grass? As Babbitts said, he must have been afraid to move, must have cowered there and seen the racer glide away and then come back; and still bent behind the network of twigs have watched the man at the wheel, as he looked up and down the road, waited and listened, every now and then sounding the horn, that broke into the silence like a weird, hollow cry.

"Oh, come on," I said suddenly, seizing Babbitts' arm. "Let's go up to Cresset's where it's bright and cheerful."

We had a lovely time at Cresset's. My, but they were a nice family! Farmer Cresset, a big, kind, jolly man and his two sons, splendid, sun-burned chaps, and his little daughter, as fresh as a peach and as shy as a kitten. I loved them all, and Mrs Cresset best. She made me think of my mother, not that she looked like her, but I guess because she had something about her that's about all women who've had families they loved.

They gave us tea and cake and they joked Babbitts good and hard about coming out there and pretending to be a tourist.

"Never mind, son," Farmer Cresset said, "you got it out of the old woman. I couldn't make her tell; seemed like she thought she'd be arrested for the crime if she up and confessed about that feller."

It was getting on for evening when we left to go to the Wayside Arbor. We'd planned to have our supper there and then go back by the branch line, catching a train at the Crossing at eight-thirty. The Cressets were real sorry to have us go, especially there.

"It ain't a nice place," said Mrs Cresset, as she kissed me goodbye, "but we're hoping to see it cleared out soon. Tom's stirring Heaven and earth to get Hines' license revoked."

"I guess Heaven's lending a hand," said the farmer, "for I hear Hines' business is bad since the fatality. We've a lot of foreign labor round here and they're mighty superstitious and are giving his place the go-by."

It was dark when we saw the lights of the Wayside Arbor, shining out across the road. We'd expected a moon to light us home, but the clouds, though they weren't as thick as they had been, were all broken up into little bits over the sky, like Heaven was paved with them.

The Arbor was quiet as we stepped up and opened the bar door, and there, just like on the night of the murder, was Hines, sitting by the stove reading a newspaper. He jumped up quick and greeted us very cordial and you could see he was glad to get a customer. He sure was a tough looking specimen with a gray stubble all over his chin, and a dirty sweater hanging open over a dirtier shirt that had no collar and was fastened with a fake gold button that left a black mark on his neck. If I thought his looks were bad that day in the summer I thought they were worse now, for he seemed more down and dispirited than he was then.

We asked him if we could have supper and he went out, calling to Mrs Hines, and we could hear someone clattering down the stairs and then a whispering going on in the hall. When he came back he said they'd get us a cold lunch, but they didn't keep a great deal on hand, seeing as how they hadn't much call for meals at that season.

You could see that was true. I never was in such a miserable, poverty-stricken hole. Leaving Babbitts talking to Hines in the bar, I went back into the dining-room, a long, shabby place that crossed the rear of the house. It was as dingy as the rest of it, with the paper all smudged and peeling off the walls and worn bits of carpet laid over the board floor. At the back two long windows looked out on the garden. Glancing through these I could see the arch of the arbor, with the wet shining on the tables and a few withered leaves trembling on the vines.

When I turned back to the room I got a queer kind of scare – a thing I would have laughed at anywhere else, but in that house on that night it turned me creepy. There was a long, old-fashioned mirror on the opposite wall with a crack going straight across the middle of it. As I caught my reflection in it, I raised my head, wanting to get the effect of my new hat, and it brought the crack exactly across my neck. Believe me I jumped and then stood staring, for it looked just as if my throat was cut! Then I moved away from it, pulling up my collar, ashamed of myself but all the same keeping out of range of the mirror.

In the bar I could hear the voices of Babbitts and Hines, Hines droning on like a person who's complaining. From behind a door at the far end of the room came a noise of crockery and pans and then a woman's voice, peevish and scolding, and another woman's answering back. I don't think I ever was in a place that got on my nerves so and what with the cold of the room – it was like a barn with no steam and the stove not lit – I sat all hunched up in my coat thinking of Sylvia Hesketh coming *there* for shelter!

Suddenly the door at the end of the room opened and Mrs Hines came in. She was the match of it all, with her red nose and her little watery eyes and her shoes dropping off at every step so you could hear the heels rapping on the boards where the carpet stopped. She began talking in a whining voice, and as she set the table, told me how the business had gone off, and they didn't know what they were going to do.

Her hands, all chapped and full of knots like twigs, smoothed out the cloth and put on the china so listless it made you tired to look at them. It was better talking to her than sitting dumb with no company but dismal thoughts, so I encouraged her and between her trailings into the kitchen and her trailings out I heard all about their affairs.

For a while after the murder they'd done a lot of business – it made me sort of shrivel up to see she didn't mind that; anything that brought trade was all the same to her – but now, nothing was doing. Only a few automobiles stopped there and the farmhands had dropped off, so their custom hardly counted. And Tecla Rabine, the Bohemian servant, who was a first-class girl, if she did have grouchy spells, had got so slack she'd have to be fired, and she, Mrs Hines, didn't see how she was to get another one what with the low wages and the lonesomeness.

She trailed off into the kitchen again and I could hear her snapping at someone and that other woman's voice growling back. I supposed it was Tecla Rabine, though it didn't sound like her, my memory of her at the inquest being of a fat, good natured thing that wouldn't have growled at anybody. And then the door was opened with one swift kick and Tecla came in, carrying a plate of bread in one hand and a platter with ham on it in the other. She didn't look grouchy at all, but gave me that broad, silly sort of smile I remembered and put the things down on the table!

"Well, Tecla," I asked for something to say, "how are *you* getting on?"

"Ach!" she answered disgusted, and pounded over the creaky floor to a cupboard out of which she took some dishes. "Me? I get out. What for do I stay? No luck here, no money. Who comes – nobody. Everything goes on the blink."

She put the things on the table and then stood looking at me, squinting up her little eyes and with her big body, in a dirty white blouse and a skirt that didn't meet it at the waist, slouched up against the table.

"I heard business was bad," I said, and thought that in spite of her being such a coarse, fat animal, she was rosy and healthy looking, which was more than you could say for the other two.

"What do I get?" she said, spreading out her great red hands, "not a thing. Maybe five, ten cents. Every long time maybe a quarter. Since that lady gets killed all goes bad. The dagoes say 'evil eye.' They walk round the house that way," she made a half-circle in the air with her arm, "looking at it afraid. Me, too, I don't like it."

"It sure is awful dismal," I agreed.

"No good," she said. "Last year this time all the rooms full – tonight – *one* man" – she held up a finger in the air – "one only man, and he have lost what makes us to laugh. When I see him, I say, 'Hein, Tito, good luck now you come. Make the bear to dance.' And he says this way" – she hunched up her shoulders and pushed out her hands the way the Guineas do – "'Oh, Gawda, there is no more bear; he makes dead long time.'"

"Bear?" I said, and then I remembered. "You mean the one that went round with the acrobats. It's dead, is it?"

Tecla nodded.

"Gone dead in the country. And he says he starve now with no bear to get pennies. The boss says we all starve, and gave him a drink and cheese and bread. Ach!" – she shook her head, as if the loss of the bear was the last straw – "I no can stand it – nothing doing, no money, no more laughs – I quit."

I didn't blame her. If you gave me two hundred a month I wouldn't have stayed there.

Just then Babbitts came in and we began our supper; cold ham and stale bread and coffee that I know was the morning's heated over. Tecla went into the kitchen and I said to him, low and guarded:

"What's Hines been saying to you?"

He answered in the same key:

"Oh, putting up a hard luck story. Cresset needn't bother. He wants to pull up stakes and go West."

"Will they let him?"

"That's one of the things he's been talking about. He says if he makes a move it'll look suspicious, and if he stays he'll be ruined. He certainly is up against it."

I shot a glance from the kitchen to the bar door and then leaned across the table, almost whispering:

"I don't see that our investigations have got us anything but a bad supper."

"Neither do I," he whispered back. "The place looks like a stage setting for The Bandits' Den, but the people don't impress me that way at all."

The kitchen door swung back and Mrs Hines came in with a pumpkin pie that tasted like it was baked for Thanksgiving. She hovered round, fussing about us and joining in the conversation. You could see she was hungry for someone to talk to. Both she and her husband impressed me that way, as if they were most crazy with the dreariness of the place, and were ready to fasten on anybody who'd speak civil to them and listen to their troubles.

Before we left, Babbitts went into the bar to settle up and I, remembering Tecla's complaints, called her in from the kitchen and fished a quarter out of my new purse. She was as pleased as a child, grinning all over, and wanting to shake hands with me, which I hated but couldn't avoid.

When we were once more in the road I gave a gasp of relief. I felt as if I'd crept out from under a shadow, that was gradually sinking into me, down to the marrow of my bones. The night was cold, but a different kind; fresh and clear, the smell of the damp fields in the air, and the country quiet and peaceful.

We had a good two miles before us and stepped out lively. It was dark; the clouds mottled over the sky; and in one place, where the moon was hidden, a little brightness showing through the cracks. Babbitts said he thought they'd break and that we'd have the moonlight on our way back.

All around us the landscape stretched black and still. When you got accustomed to it, you could see the outlines of the hills against the sky, one darkness set against another, and the line of the road showing faint between the edgings of bushes. We couldn't hear anything but our own footsteps, soft and padding because of the mud, and off and on the rustling of the twigs as I brushed against them. I don't remember ever being out on a quieter night, and there was something lovely and soothing about it after that horrible house.

We hadn't gone far – about ten minutes, I should think – when I suddenly clasped my wrist and felt that my purse was gone. I had taken it off to give Tecla the quarter and I remember I'd laid it on the supper table when she made me shake hands.

"Oh dear!" I said, stopping short. "What shall I do – I've left my purse there."

Babbitts stared at me through the dark.

"At Hines'?"

"Yes, on the supper table. And it's new, I'd only just bought it. Oh, I *can't* lose it."

"You needn't. We've time, but you'll have to hit up the pace. Come on quick – that's not just the place I'd select to leave a purse in."

He turned to go but I stood still. I hated going back there and it was lovely walking slowly along through the sharp chill air and the peaceful night.

"You go," I said, coaxing. "I'll saunter on and you can catch me up."

"Don't you mind being alone? Aren't you afraid?"

"Afraid?" I gave a laugh. "I'm much more afraid in that queer joint. Besides, I can't go as fast as you can and whatever happens we've got to catch that train."

"If you don't mind that's the best plan. I'll run both ways."

"Then hustle and I'll walk on slowly. But come whether you find the purse or not, for that's the last train to the Junction tonight, and we mustn't lose it."

"Right you are, and we won't lose anything, the train or the purse. I'll make it a rush order. Go slow till I come."

He turned and went off at a run and I walked on. At first I could hear the thud of his feet quite plainly and then the sound was suddenly deadened and I knew he was on the moist turf by the roadside. The silence closed down around me like a black curtain that seemed to be shutting me off from the rest of the world. I walked on slowly, gathering my skirts up from the wet and the twigs, as noiseless as a shadow in the dark of the trees.

I don't know how much further I went, but not very far because I could just make out the line of the Firehill Road curving down between the fields, when I heard behind me a fitful, stealthy rustling in the bushes.

XVII

In beginning this chapter, which is going to end my story of the Hesketh Mystery, I want to say right here that I'm no coward. The reason that things happened as they did was that I was worn out – more than I knew – by the strain and excitement of the last two months. Also I do think that most any girl would have lost her nerve if she'd been up against what I was.

The gloom of that dreadful Wayside Arbor was still on me as I walked along with Babbitts. After a few moments I thought it had gone off and when I told him I wasn't afraid I said what seemed to me the truth. But when the sound of his footsteps died away, the loneliness crept in on me, seemed to be telling me something that I didn't want to hear. Down deep I knew what it was, and that every step was taking me closer to what I was afraid of – the place where Sylvia Hesketh had been murdered.

It was when I was peering out ahead, trying to locate it, telling myself not to be a fool and gathering up my courage, that I heard that faint, stealthy rustling behind me.

I stopped dead, listening. I was scared but not clear through yet, for I knew it might be some little animal, a rabbit or a chipmunk, creeping through the underbrush. I stood waiting, feeling that I was breathing fast, and as still as one of the telegraph poles along the road. The trees hid me completely. A person could have passed close by and not seen me standing there in my black cloak against the black background.

Then I heard it again, very soft and cautious, a crackle of branches and then a wait, and presently – it seemed hours – a crackle of branches again. I moved forward, stepping on tiptoe, stifling my breath, my head turned sideways, listening, listening with every nerve. Even then I wasn't so terribly frightened, but I was shivery, shivery down to my heart, for I could hear that, whether it was beast or human, it was on the other side of the trees, just a little way back, going the way I was.

It only took a few minutes – me stealing forward and it coming on, now soft as it stepped on the earth, now with a twig snapping sharp – to tell me I was being followed.

When I got that clear, the last of my courage melted away. If it had been anywhere else, if it hadn't been so dark, if there'd been a house or a person within call, but, oh, Lord, in that lonesomeness, far off from everything – it was awful! And the awfullest part was that right there in front of me, getting nearer every minute, was the place where another girl had been murdered on a night like this.

I tried to pull myself together, to remember that Babbitts would be back soon, but I couldn't stop my heart from beating like a hammer, terrible thuds up in my throat. Way off through the trees I could see the twinkle of Cresset's lights and I thought of them there; but it was as if they were at the other end of the world, too far for me to reach them or for them to hear my call.

I don't know why I walked on, but I think it was pure fear. I was afraid if I stopped that dreadful following thing would overtake me. Once I tried to look back but I couldn't. I thought I might see it and I stole forward, now and then stopping and listening and every time hearing the crackle and snap of the twigs as it crept after me. I could see now the place where Sylvia was found, the shrubs curving back from the road as if to leave a space wide enough for her body.

The sight made me stop and, as I stood there still as a statue, I heard the sounds behind me get louder, as if a big body was feeling and pushing its way between the trees, not so careful now, but trampling and crushing through the interlaced boughs. Then for the first time in my life I knew what it means when they say your hair stands on end. Down at the roots of mine there was a stirring all over my head and my heart! It was banging against my chest, blow after blow, as if it was trying to break a hole.

The sky began to brighten. I got a sort of impression of those cracks in the clouds parting and the moonlight leaking through; but I didn't seem to see it plain, everything in me was turned to terror. The noise behind me was closer and louder and through it I heard a breathing, deep, panting breaths, drawn hard. Then I knew if I turned I could have seen what was following me, seen its awful face, glaring between the branches and its bent body, crouched, ready to spring.

It's hard for me to tell what followed – everything came together and I couldn't see or think. I remember trying to scream, to give one shriek for Babbitts, and no sound coming, and that the thing, as if it knew what I was doing, made a sudden crashing close at my back. The brightness of the sky flashed in my eyes. I saw the clouds broken open, and the moon, big and white, whirling round like a silver plate. I tried to run but the earth rose up in waves and I staggered forward over them, wave after wave, with the moon spinning close to my eyes, and then blackness shutting down like the lid of a box.

The next thing I remember was the sky with clouds all over it and in one place an opening with a little star as big as a pinhead set in the middle. I looked at that star for a long time, having a queer feeling that I was holding on to it and it was pulling me up. Then I felt as if something was helping the star, a strong support under my shoulders that raised me still further, and while I seemed to be struggling out of a darkness like water, I heard Babbitts' voice close to my ear:

"Thank God, she's coming out of it."

I turned my head and there was his face close to mine. A strong yellow light shone on it – afterward I saw it came from a lantern on the ground – and without speaking I looked into his eyes, and had a lovely feeling of rest as if I'd found something I was looking for.

"You're all right?" he said; "you're not hurt?"

"I'm very well, thank you," I said back, and my voice was like a whisper.

The support under my shoulders tightened, drew me up against him, and he bent down and kissed me.

We said no more, but stayed that way, looking at each other. I didn't want to move or speak. I didn't feel anything or care about anything. It seemed like Babbitts and I were the only two people in the whole world, as if there *was* no world, just us, and all the rest nothing.

After that – he's often told me it was only a minute or two, though if you'd asked me I'd have said it was hours – I began to look round and take notice. I heard queer sounds as if someone was groaning in pain, and saw the shrubs and grass plain by the light of two lanterns standing on the ground. Near these was a man, lit up as far as his knees, and close by him, all crumpled on the earth, another person. The lanterns threw a bright glow over the upper part of that figure, and I saw the head and shoulders, the hair with leaves and twigs in it and round the neck a red bandanna. Then I made out it was a man and that it was from him the sounds were coming – moans and groans and words in a strange language.

"What is it?" I whispered to Babbitts. "What's happened?"

And he whispered back:

"I'll tell you later. You're all right – that's all that matters now."

It was like a dream and I can only tell it that way – me noticing things in little broken bits, as if I was at the "movies" and kept falling to sleep, and then woke up and saw a new picture. The man who was standing turned round and it was Hines. He looked across the road and gave a shout and others answered it, and lights danced up and down, coming closer through the dark. Then men came running – Farmer Cresset and his sons – and behind them Mrs Hines, with her clothes held up high and her thin legs like a stork's. I could hear them breathing as they raced up and one man's voice crying:

"It's all right, is it? There ain't been no harm done?"

After that the men were in a group talking low, the lanterns in their hands sending circles and squares of light over the bushes and the grass. Presently Farmer Cresset broke away and went to the figure on the ground. He tried to pull him up, but the man squirmed out of his hand and fell back like a meal sack, his face to the earth, the moans coming from him loud and awful.

After a while they put me on something long and hard with a bundle under my head and took me away up the road and through the woods. It was dark and no one said anything, the Cresset boys carrying what I was on and Babbitts walking alongside. As we started I heard someone say the Farmer would stay with Hines and "communicate with the authorities." And then we went swinging off under the trees, the footsteps of the men squashing in the mud. Soon there were lights twinkling through the branches, and just as I saw them and heard a dog bark, and a woman call out, my heart faded away again and that blackness swept over me.

I didn't know till afterwards how long I was sick – weeks it was – lying in Mrs Cresset's spare room with that blessed woman caring for me like her own daughter. No people in this world were ever better to another than that family was to me. And others were good – it takes sickness and trouble to make you value human nature – for when I got desperate bad Dr Fowler came over and took a hand. Mrs Cresset herself told me that respecting Dr Graham as she did, she thought I'd never have come through if Dr Fowler hadn't given himself right up to it, staying in the house for two days the time I was worst. And not a cent would he ever take for it, only a pair of bed slippers I knitted for him while I was getting better.

It was not till I was well along on the upgrade that I heard what happened on that gruesome night. I was still in bed, sitting up in a pink flannel jacket that Anne Hennessey gave me, with the sunlight streaming in through the windows and a bunch of violets scenting up the room. Babbitts had brought them and it was he that told me, sitting in a rocker by the bedside and speaking very quiet and gentle so as not to give me any shock. For without my knowledge, just like an instrument of fate, it was I that had solved the Hesketh mystery.

Neither man nor woman had killed Sylvia Hesketh. The murderer was the dancing bear.

The man they found on the ground beside me that night was its owner, Tito Malti, the dago I had seen nearly three months before making the bear dance at Longwood, and the man Babbitts and I had seen that afternoon on the hill. Hines and Farmer Cresset carried him – he was unable to walk at first – to the Wayside Arbor and in the bar there he told them his story.

He had been associated with the acrobats for several years, working over the country with them during the summer and lying up in small towns for the winter. That spring, when the company went out on their tour, he had noticed that his bear (he called it Bruno and spoke of it like a human) showed signs of bad temper. It was a big strong beast, but was getting old and a viciousness that it had always had was growing on it. He kept quiet about it as he hoped to get through the season without trouble and knew, if the company thought it was dangerous, they wouldn't stand for having it around. All the summer he wandered with them, guarding the bear carefully, never leaving it unmuzzled, and sleeping beside it at night.

Toward the end of the season it began to grow worse. It had tried to attack one of the acrobats and there had been a quarrel. He saw he'd have to part from them, but they patched up the fight and he stayed on for their last performance at Longwood, where the business was always good.

After that they separated, the company going into winter quarters at Bloomington and Malti telling them he would take Bruno across country and make a little extra money at the farms and villages. He did intend to do this but he really wanted to get off by himself, watch the animal, and try and gain his old control over it.

He started, working round by the turnpike, letting Bruno perform when he seemed good tempered, but a good part of the time being afraid to. In this way he made enough money to keep himself, sleeping when the nights were bad, in barns and on the lee side of hayricks, the bear chained to him.

On the night of the murder he had got round as far as the Wayside Arbor. His intention had been to take his supper there – he knew the place well – and have the bear dance for the Italian customers. But by the time he reached the Arbor he didn't dare. For some days Bruno had been sullen and savage – that afternoon Malti had had to beat him with the iron-spiked staff he always carried. The poor man said he was half crazy with fright and misery. He told Hines and Cresset, who said he was as simple as a young child, that between his fear of getting into trouble with the authorities and his fear of losing the bear which was all he had in the world, he was distracted.

In the afternoon he had begged some food at a farm and with this in his pocket he tracked across the fields and woods to the turnpike near the Firehill Road. Here – it being a lonely spot – he sat down in the shade of the trees that hid him from the highway and ate his supper. As he had been on the tramp for days he was dropping with fatigue and, seeing the bear seemed quiet, he stretched out and with the chain in his hand, had fallen asleep.

He was wakened by a scream – the most awful he had ever heard. Half asleep as he was, he leaped to his feet, feeling in the dark for the chain. It was gone and the bear with it.

The scream had come from the other side of the trees. With his staff in his hand he burst through them and in the darkness saw dimly the shape of that fearful, great beast reared upon its hind legs, with a black thing lying at its feet. He yelled and struck it in the face with the staff and it dropped down to all fours, growling and terrible, but as if the sound of his voice and the blows had cowed it. Then he grabbed for the chain, moving along the ground like a snake, and holding it, knelt and looked at the black thing – the thing the scream had come from.

He raised it and saw the faint white of the face and hands and felt by the clothes it was a woman. He knew the way an enraged bear attacks – rising up to its hind legs and giving a blow with its paw, a blow that if the body it strikes is unprotected, can break bones and tear muscles out of their place. In the dark he felt the woman till his hand came on the trickle of blood on her face. That told him the brute had struck at her head, and sick and trembling, he lit a match and held it low over her. The hat had protected her from the claws; without it they would have torn through the scalp like the teeth of a rake. But when he saw her face and felt of her pulse, he knew that that savage blow had broken her skull and she was dead.

At first he was too paralyzed to think, kneeling there beside her with the bear crouched at the end of his chain, not stirring as if it was scared at what it had done. Then the horn of the Doctor's auto woke him and, clutching the body, he drew back into the shadow. The car passed at furious speed, its noise drowning any sound that that strange and awful group might have made. Shaking in every limb he laid his burden on the grass and tried to compose it, putting back the hat which was torn off, but was caught to the hair by its long pin.

While he was doing this the clouds broke and he was drawing the coat about her when the moon came out bright as day. By its light he saw the pearl necklace and in his own words, "All the badness in his heart came up into his head."

When he told that part of his story he wrung his hands and sobbed, declaring over and over that he was an honest man and a good Catholic. Never before had he stolen, though often he had gone cold and hungry. But he knew now that he must kill the bear, and then he would be left an old man without a penny or any way to earn one. "And the pearls," he moaned out, "what are they to the dead? And to me, who must live, they mean riches forever."

He said his hands shook so he couldn't find the clasp and to get at it he pulled open the coat. And then he gave a cry and drew back like he was burnt, for there on the breast of the dead woman, sparkling like a thing of fire, was the cross.

Babbitts said the two men were greatly impressed by the way he acted when he told this. The perspiration broke out on his face and he crossed himself, bowing his head and shuddering. "It was God's voice," he whispered. "It said: 'Stop, Tito; hold your hand. No man can rob the dead.'"

So he closed the coat, folded the arms across the chest and covered all with branches he found in a pile near by. As he moved about the bear watched him, not stirring, as if it knew it was guilty and was waiting to see what he would do to it.

When the work was finished the two of them stole away, as noiseless as shadows. His head was clear enough to think of the footprints and he kept on the grass till he was near the Firehill Road. He was approaching this when he heard Reddy's horn, and with the bear following, he slipped through a break in the trees into the open space beyond. Here, huddled into the blackness under the boughs, he saw the car swing past. It went a little way down the road and then stopped and stood for what seemed to him a long time, every now and then the horn sounding. When it finally started again he moved on, the bear padding silently beside him. He said the car came back soon and passed and repassed him a number of times. Each time he was ready for it, the noise and the lamps warning him of its approach. Crowded up against the bear, he watched it through the branches, all the road bright in front of it where the lamps threw their two long shoots of light.

When they asked him if he wasn't afraid of the bear making some sound he shook his head and said just like a child:

"Bruno? No – he is wise like a man. When I look him in the eye I see he knows he is a murderer and must die, and it makes him very quiet."

He had made up his mind to kill Bruno. As he told the men about it the tears ran down his face, for he said the bear was like his brother. When Reddy had gone, he made off, Bruno walking at the end of the chain behind him, both keeping to the grass edges of the fields. All night they walked, those two – and strange they must have looked slipping across the moonlit spaces, two black shadows moving over the lonesomeness, not a sound from either of them, one leading the other to his execution.

At dawn they entered the woods. There, when the light was clear enough to see, that poor, scared dago killed the bear with the knife he had carried all summer. The rest of the day he spent scooping a grave for him. When he told how he dragged the great body into the hole and covered it with earth, he put his hands over his face, rocking back and forth, and crying like a baby.

After that he went to Bloomington and joined the acrobats, telling them the bear had died. They thought no more about it and welcomed him back, sharing their quarters with him and promising him a place with them in the summer.

But his knowledge of the crime haunted him. Like all those dagoes, he was superstitious and full of queer notions. Babbitts said he was as ignorant as the animal he was so fond of, seeming to think as they couldn't hang the bear they might hang him in its place. He wanted to go to the priest and confess, but when he heard people talking of the murder he was afraid. After a while he couldn't eat or sleep and the torment of his terror and remorse was like to drive him crazy.

Finally he couldn't stand it any more and got the idea that if he could go back to the place and offer up prayers there he might get some relief. He told the acrobats he was going to hunt for work on a farm, left Bloomington and once again walked across the country.

It was night when he reached the region he was bound for, and feeling too weak and sick to go straight to the spot, he went to the Wayside Arbor to beg for food which would give him strength to bear the task he had set himself. They gave him what he asked for and he took it to his old nook under the trees and there in the cold and dark ate ravenously. Then, just as on that other night, he lay down and the sleep that had left him for so long came back to him.

He never heard us pass, but I guess without his knowing it we wakened him, for he said he was sitting up, rubbing his eyes, when he heard Babbitts' footsteps as he ran back to the inn.

He listened and, making sure no one else was on the road, got up and began to steal cautiously forward. He felt sure that God would hear his prayers after he had walked so far and his misery had been so great.

I guess the poor thing was about all in, and was as scared when he came near the place as I was. Of course he had no idea I was in front of him and wasn't following me as I thought. With the trees between, both of us were making for the same spot, the only difference being that while I heard him he never heard me.

What he saw when he broke through the hedge would have terrified anyone, let alone a man in the state he was. For there, just as he had last seen her, lay a woman in a black coat with the moonlight shining on her dead white face – a ghost waiting to accuse him.

They say the shriek he gave was the most awful that man ever heard. Babbitts, who was on his way back, said it sounded like it came from a lost soul in Hell. He tried to yell back, but couldn't and ran like a madman, and when he got there saw me lying as if I was dead in the moonlight and a wild, screaming figure crouched on the ground beside me. The two Hines heard it. Hines picked up a lantern and ran with Mrs Hines at his heels. When he came up he found Babbitts kneeling over me, half crazy, thinking I was murdered, too. They felt my pulse and found it was going and sent Mrs Hines on the run to Cresset's. She lit out, calling and crying as she flew through the woods, and met the Cresset crowd, hiking along with their lanterns, having heard her and not knowing *what* had happened.

Well – that's the end of my story. Oh, I forgot the reward – *I* got it. I oughtn't to have for I didn't do anything but fall in a faint, which was the easiest thing I could do. But Mrs Fowler and the Doctor wouldn't have it any other way, so I gave in. Not that I didn't want to. Believe me, Jew or Gentile gets weak when ten thousand dollars is pressed into her palm. It's invested and I get good interest on it, but I'm saving that up. You never can tell what may happen in this world.

As to the rest of us – the bunch that in one way or another were drawn into the Hesketh mystery – we're all scattered now.

Jack Reddy's not living at Firehill any more. He's taken an apartment in town where the two old Gilseys look after him like he was their only son, and he's studying law in Mr Whitney's office. Sometimes Sunday he comes to see us, just as cordial and kind and handsome as ever, and it's I that'll be glad when he tells me he's found the right girl – God bless him!

Cokesbury Lodge is sold and Cokesbury's living in town, too. They say his part in the Hesketh case sort of finished him. High society wouldn't stand for it, which shows you can't believe all you hear about the idle rich. I've heard that he's seen round a lot with an actress-lady and one of the papers had it he was going to marry her.

The Fowlers went to Europe. They're living in Paris now and I hear from Anne Hennessey, who corresponds with Mrs Fowler, that they're going to reside there. Anyway, Jim Donahue told me last time I was down at Longwood that Mapleshade was to let.

Annie's got a new job in town, on Fifth Avenue, grand people who never quarrel. She dines with us most every Sunday and we sit till all hours talking over the past, like people who've been in some great disaster and when they get together always drift back to the subject.

Me? – you want to know about me?

Well, I'm living uptown on the West Side in the cutest little flat in New York – five rooms, on a corner, all bright and sunny. And furnished! Say, I wish I could show them to you. When Mrs Fowler broke up she gave me a lot of the swellest things. Why, I've got a tapestry in the parlor that cost five hundred dollars and cut glass you couldn't beat on Fifth Avenue.

It's on 125th Street, near the Subway. We had to be near that for Himself – he likes to stay as late as he can in the morning and get up as quick as he can at night. If you're passing that way any time, just drop in. I'd love to see you and have you see my place – and me, too. You'll see the name on the letter-box – Morganthau? Oh, quit your kidding – it's *Babbitts* now.